Tanner reached over and touched her arm, just below her elbow. "Do *you* need anything, Bree? Tell me what's going on. I can help."

She looked into his eyes and almost believed him. Was tempted, maybe, because of the exhaustion, to tell him at least *something*. Not everything, of course, but enough to get his help.

He looked so strong. So capable. Like he could handle anything. While she woke every day not sure how she was going to make it, each day worse than the one before.

He waited silently, not pushing, not demanding. Which just made her want to lean on him more.

But she couldn't. She couldn't depend on anyone but herself.

CALCULATED RISK

USA TODAY Bestselling Author

JANIE CROUCH

To the Chamblee High School Class of 1965 (and thereabouts)—my mother's graduating class. Thank you for letting me borrow your names.

ISBN-13: 978-1-335-60446-0

Calculated Risk

Recycling programs for this product may not exist in your area.

This edition published by arrangement with Harlequin Books S.A.

For questions and comments about the quality of this book, please contact us at CustomerService@Harlequin.com.

Printed in U.S.A.

Janie Crouch has loved to read romance her whole life. This *USA TODAY* bestselling author cut her teeth on Harlequin Romance novels as a preteen, then moved on to a passion for romantic suspense as an adult. Janie lives with her husband and four children overseas. She enjoys traveling, long-distance running, movie watching, knitting and adventure/obstacle racing. You can find out more about her at janiecrouch.com.

Books by Janie Crouch

Harlequin Intrigue

The Risk Series: A Bree and Tanner Thriller

Calculated Risk

Omega Sector: Under Siege

Daddy Defender
Protector's Instinct
Cease Fire

Omega Sector: Critical Response

Special Forces Savior
Fully Committed
Armored Attraction
Man of Action
Overwhelming Force
Battle Tested

Omega Sector

Infiltration
Countermeasures
Untraceable
Leverage

Primal Instinct

Visit the Author Profile page at Harlequin.com.

CAST OF CHARACTERS

Tanner Dempsey—Deputy captain of the sheriff's office in Grand County, Colorado, who lives and works in Risk Peak.

Bree Daniels—Computer genius on the run from the Organization, a terrorist group that funnels information.

Melissa Weather—Bree's cousin, desperately in need of Bree's help.

Ronnie Kitchens—Sheriff's deputy in Risk Peak.

Michael Jeter—Head of the Organization and public face of the Communication for All charity group.

Cheryl and Dan Andrews—Owners of the Sunset Diner in Risk Peak.

Scott Watson—Member of sheriff's office intercounty task force on communication, temporarily stationed in Risk Peak.

Bill Steele—Construction worker in Risk Peak.

Chapter One

Bree Daniels froze, fork halfway to her mouth, at the sound of the knock at her apartment door. She forced herself to put the fork down slowly and remain calm.

A knock on the door wasn't a cause for panic for most people. But from the time Bree was twelve, she'd been taught that danger of the most deadly kind could wait on the other side of any door.

She took a deep breath and let it out.

It wasn't that no one ever knocked on her door. She regularly ordered things that had to be delivered. As a matter of fact, most of her shopping was done online. Everything from clothing to groceries. Buying what she needed on the internet meant less interaction with people and no need to leave her downtown Kansas City apartment.

But Bree always knew exactly—usually to the hour—when the items would arrive. When a knock would come on her door.

This was not one of those times.

She waited, hoping it was just some kid or lost person who would go away, tensing when a second knock came. She stood, moving toward the emergency bug-out bag she kept packed in the coat closet. It contained everything she needed for a quick getaway: clothing, a wad of cash, a few items that could be used to change her appearance and a fake ID she'd never used.

She hadn't needed the bag since arriving here three years ago on her twenty-first birthday. She didn't want to use it now unless she absolutely had to. Despite the wisdom of it, she loved this little apartment. It had become home. She didn't want to leave.

A woman's voice came from the other side of the door.

"Bethany?"

Now Bree ran for the closet. It was definitely time for the bug-out bag.

Nobody knew her by the name Bethany. At least, no one who wanted her alive.

Another soft knock. Another whisper at the door. "Please, Bethany. I don't have anywhere else to go."

Bree didn't stop, just grabbed the bag and ran toward the window in the living room. The fire escape outside her second-floor apartment was the reason she had chosen this unit in the first place.

Always have multiple exits. Always have a plan.

And she did. To get the hell out. She was climbing through the window when she heard the words from the door.

"Crisscross, applesauce."

Bree froze. No, it couldn't be. She hadn't heard those words, the code she'd shared with her cousin when they were younger, in more than a decade.

Melissa had been the only person Bree had ever truly opened up to, the only person who'd taken the time to try to understand the socially awkward Bethany. Their upbringing had been isolated and cold—before Bree's had turned into a total nightmare—but together it had been bearable.

Crisscross, applesauce.

That phrase had been their agreed-upon code, hidden from the Organization, to let each other know if they were truly in need.

They were quite possibly the only words in the world that could've stopped Bree from crawling out that window and leaving here forever.

Was it a trap?

If Bree's mother was still alive, she would've definitely said yes. They would've already been out the window and moving to separate locations to meet up later if it was safe. That had always been their agreed-upon plan, even when it meant Bree had to spend a week living by herself when she was fourteen. Whatever kept them alive.

Knowing she might be making the worst mistake of her life, that her mother was probably rolling over in her grave, Bree stopped and turned back toward her front door.

Saying a quick prayer and calling herself all sorts of stupid, she cracked open the door.

She knew immediately it was Melissa. She was more than a decade older than when Bree had last seen her at thirteen, but her features and long blond hair were still the same. Bree had been so jealous of Mel's beautiful curls when they were kids. Her own straight brown hair had seemed so boring in comparison.

She'd made a mistake by opening the door. Even if

Melissa wasn't here because she meant to kill her—and Bree still wasn't sure of that—Melissa was part of a life Bree wanted nothing to do with.

"I'm sorry, you've got the wrong place. There's nobody by that name here." Bree quickly shut the door.

"Bethany, I know it's you. Please, it's Melissa. I'm not going to hurt you, and I haven't told anybody in the Organization where you are. But I need your help."

Bree rested her forehead against the door. It had been so long since…everything. Since seeing Melissa. Since hearing anyone call her by her real name.

Since talking to anyone person to person at all.

"Crisscross, applesauce. Crisscross, applesauce." Melissa kept softly saying it over and over against the door.

Shaking her head, Bree opened it again.

"Oh, God, thank you," Melissa said before Bree yanked her inside. Immediately Bree started patting down her cousin, looking for a weapon. Not finding one didn't make her feel any better. If the other woman was here to betray Bree, she wouldn't be here alone.

"I don't have any guns," Melissa said as Bree finished the pat down. "And I don't have very much time."

"Why are you here, Mel?"

Bree stood stiff as her cousin threw her arms around Bree's torso. She couldn't remember the last time someone had hugged her. Her mom had stopped long before she died.

"Why are you here?" she asked again. "How did you find me?"

Melissa stepped back. "I discovered you were in

Kansas City a few months ago. But only recently did I find this place."

Bree tried to focus on what Melissa was saying and not on the fear coursing through her system. If Melissa could find her, so could the rest of the Organization.

Melissa grabbed her hands. "Nobody knows but me. I promise. I need your help, Bethany."

"Bree," she said automatically. "I go by Bree now."

"Bree. It suits you." Melissa gave her a small smile, her hands wringing. "I don't have much time. It won't take them long to figure out I'm gone. They're suspicious already."

Bree watched her closely, still ready to run if needed. "What do you need?"

"I found out the truth about the Organization. I want to get out. I've wanted to for a long time, but now I think I have the means."

Bree shut her eyes and shook her head. "I—"

"Things are so much worse now than when you were there. The things they can do now…"

Bree didn't want to get drawn back into this. She was already going to have to run again. The thought of leaving this place hurt. "I can't help you. Honestly, I'm not in any position to help *anyone*. And if you know I'm here, the Organization does, too."

Melissa grabbed Bree's hand, and she fought not to flinch away. "No, they don't know. They may know I'm here, but they don't know it's *you*. And I have a couple of allies on the inside now. People who can be trusted."

The only person Bree trusted was herself. When it came to the Organization, the price on her head was too high to trust anybody.

The phone in Melissa's hand pinged, and she let out a curse.

"I'm out of time." Her features became more pinched. "There's so much I need to tell you. Please, Bethany—*Bree*—please meet me tonight so I can explain everything. There's so much more at stake than you could ever dream, than *I* could've ever dreamed. I have to make my move now or I'll lose everything." Desperation dripped from every word.

"Mel, I just don't think—"

"Just meet me tonight," Melissa cut her off. "At the downtown train station at midnight. I'll bring the hard drive. It has everything we need to truly get our freedom. I'll show you why it's critical I make my move now."

When the phone in her hand beeped again, Melissa bolted to the door. She turned, eyes entreating. "Criss-cross, applesauce, Bethany. Please."

All Bree could do was watch her go.

TWELVE HOURS LATER, at almost midnight, Bree sat in her car in a location giving her good visual access to the train station.

She was making a mistake. She *knew* she was making a mistake, that this was all going to end badly…yet here she was.

She'd been watching the station for the past two hours, looking for any sign that Melissa had set her up, that this was a trap and the Organization would be moving in to capture Bree.

She'd found no indication at all that that was the case.

Just like she'd found no indication of betrayal after

she'd immediately vacated her apartment this afternoon when Melissa left. As far as Bree could tell—and she'd become very proficient at the tactical skill of observation—no one had been watching or following her all day.

It disturbed her slightly how much she wanted to believe her cousin's intentions were good. Even if it went against the idea her mother had spent so many years instilling: *no one* could be trusted.

In the end, her mother hadn't even trusted Bree. She rubbed the raised flesh of the knife scar on her shoulder under her shirt. Her mother's parting gift, before taking her own life, thinking Bree was about to do it.

But Bree had seen nothing suspicious or out of the ordinary here for hours. So she was fairly certain she was going to do the stupid thing and get out of this car to help Melissa.

Even if she knew the smart thing would've been to already be two hundred miles outside Kansas City. That's why she'd chosen the city right smack in the middle of America—she could travel in any direction if she needed to get out quick.

But the fact of the matter, and the reason Bree was sitting here right now, was that if Melissa had intended to turn over Bree to the Organization, her best bet would've been to do it earlier today when she had the element of surprise. Melissa had known her apartment number, so all she'd really needed to do was have someone guarding the fire escape and ready to catch Bree when she ran.

But Mel hadn't.

Crisscross, applesauce.

Shaking her head, Bree got out of the car and headed toward the designated parking lot to meet Melissa.

The choice of locations was a good one. Trains were accessible, of course, and the bus depot was only two blocks away. In a personal vehicle someone could be on three different major interstates in less than five minutes.

Bree kept to the shadows, circling the area and waiting for Melissa. When by fifteen minutes past their scheduled meeting time Melissa hadn't arrived, Bree began to get worried. She gave her ten more minutes after that, then knew it wasn't safe to stay in one place any longer.

Something had changed—planned or unplanned. Either way, Bree couldn't stay here. All she could do was pray her mother's voice screaming in her head hadn't been right and this was all a setup.

She had her answer a few moments later as she approached her car and felt the cold metal of a gun muzzle against the back of her neck.

Sorry, Mom, I guess you were right.

"Would've probably been less conspicuous to take me out at my apartment. Nobody knew me there anyway," she said, raising her hands to shoulder level, as if she had no plans to fight.

There weren't too many self-defense moves she could do if the shooter was going to assassinate her with a slug to the back of the head. But if he or she had instructions to bring Bree back alive, Bree would have opportunities to make her own attack. Better to make the person think she was compliant.

Bree very definitely wasn't compliant, and there was

no way in hell someone was taking her back to the Organization alive.

"Melissa sent me." A man's voice.

"Well, tell her I said she played me just right. I honestly believed she needed my help right up until the second I felt your gun at my neck."

"She does need your help. I'm not here to hurt you. Melissa was being watched, so she couldn't come herself." And then, amazingly, the cold metal eased back from her skin.

Bree turned around slowly, then blanched as she found herself looking into cold eyes she hadn't seen in over ten years.

It took every ounce of self control she had not to scurry away or whimper.

Everyone had called him Smith, although that certainly wasn't his real name. He'd been in charge of discipline. He'd been old even then. He looked ancient now.

"You know who I am?" he asked.

"Yes." How could she possibly forget the man who had broken more than one of her bones? "What I don't know is why I'm alive and still conscious."

Smith shook his head. "As I said, I'm not here to harm you. Melissa needed me to deliver important… items that are required in order for her to escape the Organization."

"You're helping her?"

"They've gone too far, even for me." He gave the smallest shrug with his shoulder. "And maybe what I'm doing here today will help make up for the sins of my past. But we don't have much time. I'll lead them away from your direction, but that's all I can do."

He pushed an old flip phone into her hand. "You hold the future now. Melissa will be in touch as soon as she can. I placed the items in the back seat of your car. Be careful. They are everything."

Bree turned toward her car. *They* were everything? She turned back toward the caretaker. "What are you talking about—"

He was gone, disappeared into the darkness.

She shook her head and turned back toward her car—a nondescript late-model Honda most people wouldn't pay attention to—cautiously, even knowing she could've been killed multiple times over by now if that was someone's intent.

She heard yelling on the other side of the parking lot and picked up her pace. Maybe it was just the normal type of trouble that could be found in an empty downtown parking lot in the middle of the night, but maybe it was trouble coming specifically for her. She paused again as she came up on her car, seeing two large, odd-shaped boxes in the back seat.

She'd been expecting some files, but electronic ones on a hard drive. Definitely not anything that size.

After another couple steps, Bree realized those weren't file boxes at all. She ran the last few feet to her car, pushing her face up against the window.

"Oh, my God, Mel, what have you done?"

Chapter Two

Bree stared, rubbed her eyes just to make sure she hadn't been affected by some sort of airborne hallucinogen, then stared some more.

Not file boxes at all. Strapped into the back seat of her car were two separate baby carriers. Inside each of them was a tiny sleeping infant. Bree didn't know anything about babies, but those were definitely fresh ones. New. Couldn't be more than five minutes old, right?

A note was taped to the top of one of the carriers, so she carefully opened the door and grabbed it.

> I couldn't get out. But you see now why I have to. Their names are Christian and Beth, and they're two months old. The Organization doesn't know about them. I will keep it that way and hope you will keep them safe until I can escape.
>
> Crisscross, applesauce, Bree. You hold my heart in your hands every time you pull the twins close. I never knew what true family was until I had them.

Bree removed the small hard drive attached to the paper then crumpled it, bringing her fist down softly on the roof of the car. She didn't know the first thing about babies. Had never held one in her life. What was she going to do now?

She quietly shut the back door—heaven forbid she wake one of them up—and got into the driver's side. Staying here wasn't safe. Her fingers wrapped around the steering wheel in a death grip as she pulled the car out of the parking lot.

She'd known it was going to be hard. But this was so much worse than she thought.

There were babies in the back seat.

Not just one. *Two. Babies.* One of them even named after her. *Oh, Mellie.*

This changed every possible plan that had been stirring around in Bree's head since Melissa showed up this afternoon. All the routes she and Melissa could choose, modes of transportation they could take. She'd had multiple possible plans.

Prepare for the unexpected and you're much more likely to get out of a situation alive. She could almost hear her mother's voice.

But of all the scenarios Bree had run in her head, none of them had involved the particular variables she was dealing with right now. All her options were now defunct.

Because *babies.*

She glanced down at the phone Smith had given her. It wasn't a high-tech smartphone; it was a low-tech flip phone that could barely be used to make a call.

A safe phone, so low-tech that it would be difficult for the Organization to use it to find someone.

She quickly scrolled through the call history to see

if she could find any information, a way to get in touch with Melissa, let her know what a terrible plan this was, but there was nothing. Until Melissa called Bree, the phone was basically useless.

How long before Melissa could get away from the Organization? Hours? Days?

Years?

When one of the babies let out a soft gurgle from the back seat, Bree put the phone down and focused on figuring out where to go. Maybe the best plan was to go back to her apartment. Obviously, Melissa didn't intend her any harm, so Bree's home was probably safe.

At least it would allow her a chance to regroup. Figure out what she was going to do.

She knew something was wrong as soon as she drove up to her block. Her apartment was in a busy, but not dangerous, part of the city, something she'd been specifically looking for when she'd chosen the place. She'd wanted to be able to slip in and out, day or night, without people paying much attention to her. To be able to blend into a crowd instantly if needed.

There were enough units in the building that people were constantly coming and going, and it was urban enough that nobody thought much of it if you didn't stop and talk to them.

But right now it looked like every single person in the building was out on the street surrounding it. At one o'clock in the morning.

Bree parked the car on a side street. She left the twins sleeping inside, tucked most of her long brown hair up into a ball cap so it looked much shorter and then jogged over to the people at the edge of the crowd. She kept an eye on the car as she spoke to an older couple she'd seen around but had never talked to.

"Hi, I live in 4A. I just got home. What's going on? Is it a fire?"

The old man kept his arm around his wife while he shook his head at Bree. "Gas leak. They came door to door about an hour ago. Told us it would be at least five or six hours before we could get back in."

"Where's the fire department?"

The older woman shrugged. "I guess the rest of them are on their way. We only saw one. It was the gas company employees knocking on doors and checking people off their list."

Bree knew if it was dangerous enough to be taking people out of their homes in the middle of the night, it was dangerous enough to have a full firefighting crew here. This definitely wasn't right.

"So everyone just has to stand out here for five or six more hours?"

"No," the man said. "They said they'd provide rooms at a local hotel down the block for free. All you needed to do was show them your ID and let them run a credit card for any incidentals."

Bree grimaced. More likely a convenient place to herd everyone from the building and double-check their identification.

She glanced over at the car. Nobody was near it, but she needed to get the twins out of here. This had the Organization written all over it.

The older woman gave out a weary sigh. "Harold just walked down to use the ATM and couldn't get it to work. It said our account was temporarily on hold. I don't want to go to some strange hotel in my pajamas with no money."

A younger woman turned to them from a few yards away. "Did you guys say your bank account is on hold? Mine told me the same thing a few minutes ago when I went to grab some cash."

Harold let out another frustrated sigh. "Unbelievable. At First National Trust?"

The woman shook her head. "No, Bank United. Everybody's system must be down."

Or somebody was making sure that everybody in the building ended up where they were subtly being directed.

The Organization was casting a net. They didn't know what their fish looked like, so they were going to dredge everything, then sort it out.

Bree pulled her hat farther down on her head. Everything happening on the street right now—all the people gathered here—was being recorded, she was sure of it.

After all, hadn't the Organization started teaching her how to use her computer skills for surveillance when she was only ten years old? They'd taught her how to target, how to track, how to incapacitate an enemy virtually. Then used her natural abilities to further develop methods of spying and tracking.

Until her mother had realized the prestigious computer school that was supposed to be providing a young Bethany a leg up in coding and systems was actually using her abilities to further their own nefarious purposes. And had no plan to ever let her leave.

Bree spoke to Harold and the others for just a few more moments before easing herself away and walking nonchalantly back to her car and slipping inside. She started the car and pulled away slowly despite every instinct that screamed to drive as fast as she could. That would do nothing but draw attention to her. Attention she desperately could not afford.

As she passed Harold and his wife, she noticed that a man wearing a Central Gas jacket was now talking to the older couple, clipboard in hand. When Harold pointed in her direction, she dipped lower in her seat, gritting her teeth, forcing herself to hold her speed consistent.

She could feel computerized eyes on her everywhere. Every phone in this vicinity was recording—whether the owners knew it or not—and sending information back to the Organization.

If Bree made one wrong move, did anything that drew unwanted attention to herself, they would be on her in a heartbeat.

She could feel the phantom pain of her leg being broken by the Organization. Hear her own screams. Her mother's sobs.

She couldn't let them take her again. So she forced herself to remain calm, to keep her car steady and slow, even though her eyes were almost glued to the rearview mirror expecting vehicles to be chasing her any moment.

But none came.

The gas man would be asking who she was. Hopefully the couple would remember Bree said 4A. The real person from 4A was the one in the building who looked most similar to Bree. Caucasian female. Brown hair. Average height and weight. Mid- to late-twenties.

Side by side it would be obvious Bree and 4A's occupant weren't the same person, but in general description they were similar enough to buy Bree some time as they searched for the wrong person.

She was going to need every extra minute she could get. She had no doubt her accounts, like everyone else's, had been frozen. They would be unfrozen as soon as she stepped foot in a bank and showed ID. But then the Organization would have a record of her, photographs.

They would figure out she was alive, and the hunt would truly begin.

So she was trapped with just the cash she had on her. Alone, that would've lasted her six months or more. More than enough time to get established somewhere and get a new job.

As if on cue one baby began crying in the back. It wasn't long before the other was joining its sibling.

Bree definitely wasn't alone anymore.

Chapter Three

Tanner Dempsey didn't spend a lot of his time in the baby aisle of Risk Peak's lone drugstore. His sister had made him an uncle three times over in the last decade, but when he was shopping for his niece and nephews, it was in the toy department.

He didn't spend a lot of time at the drugstore at all. He was only here now at 7:00 p.m., after working a twelve-hour shift, because if he showed up at his mother's house tomorrow without shaving, he'd never hear the end of it from his siblings.

Since Tanner tended to have a five o'clock shadow about two hours after he shaved, Gary, the manager here, kept a couple packages of the special razor refill brand Tanner liked. Gary stuffed them in the back aisle so no one else would buy them.

Tanner meant to just grab the pack and run, but his attention was caught by a young mother—one crying baby in her arms, another in a car seat carrier on the ground—moving in odd, jerky movements in the baby aisle.

Tanner immediately knew the woman wasn't from around here. He'd lived in Risk Peak, Colorado, his entire life, except for the four years he'd gone to college about an hour east in Denver. Risk Peak definitely wasn't so large that he wouldn't know an attractive brunette in her twenties who'd recently had twins.

And man, that one kid had a set of lungs on him. The fact that the mother was moving so awkwardly wasn't helping calm the baby.

Tiredness pushed aside, Tanner stayed at the end of the aisle out of the woman's sight, picking up a random package and pretending to read the back of it in case she looked at him. His subterfuge probably wasn't even necessary. She was so busy with her odd movements and the crying baby, she definitely wasn't looking his way.

It didn't take him long to figure out what was going on. The woman was taking individual packets of formula out of a larger box and stuffing them wherever she could manage. In her own pockets, in the diaper bag and even inside the onesie of the crying child.

No wonder the kid was bawling.

Tanner had seen a lot in his thirty-three years, but a mother stealing formula by stuffing it in the baby's clothes? That was a first. Now he'd seen it all.

Then she opened a package of diapers and started stuffing those in with the second baby in the carrier, hidden under the blanket.

Correction. *Now* he'd seen it all.

She was watching the other end of the aisle, toward the front of the store, to make sure no one caught her. But evidently she thought the back of the store was empty, which it normally would be.

He watched her for a few more moments to make sure he understood what was going on. When she dropped the half-empty pack of diapers and was struggling to pick them up, Tanner decided he had seen enough.

"Let me get those for you." He moved quickly toward her, ignoring her startled little shriek, and grabbed the half-open package of diapers from the floor and offered them to her.

And was met by the most brilliant green eyes he'd ever seen.

It took him a second to recover enough to even take in the rest of her features. Long brown hair pulled back in a low ponytail, pert nose covered in freckles that also covered her cheeks and full sensual lips.

Kissable lips.

This was definitely a woman he would know if she lived here, whether she'd just had twins or not. Not that anyone in Risk Peak would allow a young mother to become so desperate that she had to shoplift formula and diapers.

She didn't show any sign of drug use or intoxication, as he'd half feared she would. Her eyes were clear, not at all bloodshot, and her skin, although pale since he'd just startled her, lacked the sunken pallor that so often accompanied substance abuse.

She was beautiful.

But surrounding her beauty was an air of desperation and weariness—much more than just a new mother's exhaustion. This was almost like a tangible fear.

But maybe it was because she'd just gotten busted shoplifting.

"Thank you," she muttered in a husky voice, taking the diaper package. "I was just about to pay for them, and then the package ripped open."

Tanner gave her a nod, ignoring the lie. "I'm sure handling everything with two little ones is a hardship. Is their dad around? Your husband? Someone who can help you?"

"No. No, it's just me. I don't have a husband." She looked so overwhelmed and breakable, all big eyes and crying baby. It made Tanner want to forget everything that he was, the vows he had made, and help her.

More than just help her—fight against whatever it was that was putting such fear in those green eyes. Even if that was her own bad choices.

Which was absurd, considering he'd met her thirty seconds ago and didn't even know her name.

"Maybe I can help you." He took a step forward but paused when she jerked back.

She began looking around frantically. "I just realized I don't have my purse. I—I better go get that. I'll leave the diapers here and come back for them."

She shifted the crying baby, a boy by the look of the blue outfit, into her other arm, shushing him softly and kissing his forehead. Then hefted up the baby in the carrier with her free arm. Without another word to him, she turned and walked toward the door.

Tanner was only a step behind her as she walked toward the front of the store. He wasn't sure what he was going to do. He should've made his official position known from the beginning. Mentioning it now was going to throw her into an even bigger panic.

But he wanted to help. Every instinct screamed that this was a woman at the end of her rope. He might have just caught her in the act of breaking the law, but that didn't necessarily mean she was the villain in this story.

Sometimes justice and the law weren't the same thing. Even a lawman sometimes had to break the rules if it was the right thing to do. His father had taught him that.

Of course, his father had also been killed in the line of duty.

Tanner would follow her out and make sure she made it to her car all right and wasn't in so much a hurry that she got in an accident. Then he could come back and pay for what she'd taken, and nobody had to be wiser about any of it. Gary would understand.

They were walking past the front counter, the woman throwing a worried glance at him over her shoulder every few seconds, when Gary decided to be friendly. The way he always was.

"Officer Dempsey," Gary called out. "Did you find your razor refill?"

Tanner could see every muscle in the small woman's body tense as she spun around and looked at him. "Officer?"

The baby finally stopped crying. The woman looked like she wanted to bolt but knew she wouldn't make it very far with her cargo in tow.

Tanner tilted his head toward Gary but kept his eyes on the woman. "Technically, it's captain of the southeast department of the Grand County Sheriff's Office. And yeah, Gary, I did find what I was looking for, but this lovely young mother—what's your name again?"

"Bree," she murmured.

He turned back to Gary. "Bree seems to have forgotten her wallet, and I thought I would show her a little Risk Peak hospitality and pay for the diapers and formula she needs."

She didn't say anything, just looked at him like she expected him to start reading her her rights any second.

"Here's the diaper and formula package." Tanner placed the tattered packaging on the counter. "They both…somehow ripped."

"Are you serious? I'm so sorry," Gary muttered. "If you wait just a second, miss, I'll go get you packages that aren't ripped."

She finally broke eye contact with Tanner to look at Gary. "There's no need to do that. I think half of it fell out in the baby carrier anyway."

Gary smiled and looked at the baby in her arms. "Yep, look, there's a formula packet right there in this little guy's outfit." He reached over and grabbed the small packet of formula from near the baby's neck. Bree flushed and looked away.

They stood there awkwardly as Gary rang up the items, chatting the entire time about the weather, Tanner's upcoming fly-fishing trip and the decline of the quality of plastic as evidenced by the ripped diaper and formula packages, before finally putting the items in a bag.

Bree murmured her thanks and then moved with the babies out the door.

Tanner was right behind her.

He followed her out to her gray Honda, which at least didn't look like it was going to fall apart on the side of the road. She immediately began buckling the car seats into the car.

"Were you waiting until we got out here to arrest me?" she asked when she saw he had followed her.

He leaned against her hood. "No laws were broken.

Everything was paid for before anyone exited the store. So, no need for an arrest."

She let out a sigh. "Thank you. It's very kind of you to help me. Can I pay you back?"

The tightness in her features screamed that she didn't have the money to pay him back. He was almost tempted to say yes just to see what she would do.

But his mother hadn't raised him that way. "No, there's no need."

Some of the tension faded. "Well, thanks again. I've got to get going."

He kept his posture as relaxed as possible. "There are government assistance measures in place if you can't afford what you need. If you come down to my office, we could help get you set up."

She stiffened, then shook her head. "No, it's not like that. My wallet got stolen, but I'll be fine."

Her wallet may have gotten stolen, but he had a feeling there was a lot more to it than that. "If you're in some sort of trouble, I can help."

She shook her head before walking around to the driver's side. "No, I'm fine. I just need to get to where I'm going."

"And where is that?" He hefted himself from the hood and walked toward her. She immediately took the long way around the car, keeping distance between them. She opened the driver's-side door.

"Thank you for your help," she said, not answering the question.

He sighed. "I'd like to do more."

"Well, I appreciate it, but I don't need more." She gave him a smile, but it didn't come anywhere close to meeting her eyes. All the desperation and fear he'd sensed earlier was back again. "We'll be fine and out of your hair in no time, Sheriff."

"Just captain of the department. Sheriff Duggan is my boss, although she's at the office about forty miles north of here," he corrected with a smile.

She nodded but didn't say anything further.

She was slipping through his fingers, and there wasn't a damned thing he could do about it. But since he wasn't going to arrest her and couldn't force her to come in and get help, he had to let her go.

He gripped the roof of her car and leaned toward her. "The Sunrise Diner is down the street on the way out of town. At least stop by there and grab yourself something to eat before you head out. Tell them to put in on my tab. Believe me, they'll get a hoot out of it."

Cheryl and Dan Andrews ran the place together. They'd known Tanner since he was born and would be more than thrilled to provide a meal for Bree and coo over the babies. They probably wouldn't even let him pay them back.

"Yeah, okay. Maybe."

She looked so fragile. He wanted to do more. But sometimes pushing did more harm than good.

"Good luck to you, Bree, and your babies. I hope you get to where you're going before you run out again." He wasn't just talking about running out of baby supplies.

"Me, too," she whispered. Then she got in the car and drove away.

BREE'S WHOLE BODY was shaking so badly she could barely make it out of the parking lot. If the cop hadn't been there, she wouldn't even have tried. But there was no way she could stay there and continue to talk to him.

Talking to anyone was almost impossible for her. But then to have been caught red-handed and almost been arrested? She couldn't believe she'd been so stupid.

If law enforcement got her name and ran a background check on her, the name Bree Daniels would be fine and shouldn't alert anyone in the Organization. But if they took her fingerprints and ran her through any database?

She was as good as dead.

But shoplifting had been her only option. Six weeks on the run with two newborns had depleted nearly everything of Bree's. Almost all her money. Then all her energy and stamina. And maybe now her sanity.

She felt one breath away from a breakdown.

She didn't know what to do. They'd burned through her saved money much faster than she'd anticipated. Who knew that tiny little humans could need so much *stuff*?

She'd stayed near Kansas City the first few days after the twins had been left in her care. It was a little risky, but Bree was familiar with the city and had been praying the phone Melissa had provided would ring. But it didn't.

Bree could write elaborate computer code, had an innate ability at developing software and could hack into some of the most secure databases on the planet if she wanted to.

But babies? Bree had no idea.

She wasn't good with people on any day. She definitely wasn't equipped to provide 24/7 care for two beings whose only method of communicating was screaming their heads off when they weren't happy.

Diaper changing, feeding schedules, holding, swaddling, sleeping on their back, buckling in car seats, burping…

She'd rather try to hack Department of Defense nuclear codes. It would take less time and energy.

From a purely intellectual level, Bree could understand why Melissa had chosen her to care for the babies. Bree was quite possibly the only person in the world who was living completely free of the Organization but still knew how dangerous they were. How important it was to keep away from them.

But just because she knew that didn't mean she wasn't ruining these children's lives. For six weeks Bree had barely kept the three of them above water. And things were just getting worse.

If Melissa could see them all now, both kids starting to wail from the back seat, Bree barely able to make it out of a parking lot after almost being arrested—Melissa would know she'd made the wrong choice by asking Bree to help.

She'd stayed at hotels at first, paying with cash, not realizing how much the babies would need and how much it would cost.

In the third week, low on cash, she'd made the biggest mistake of all. She'd decided to use her credit card. It wasn't under the name Bree Daniels—it wasn't under a name associated with her at all.

But in her exhaustion she forgot it had been linked to her address in Kansas City.

If they hadn't run out of diapers, forcing an emergency trip to the local supercenter in the middle of the night, she would've been there when the Organization's hired thugs came crashing into the hotel room.

As it was, she'd narrowly escaped. The number of sedans in the hotel parking lot—and the fact that her mother, in all her paranoia, had taught Bree to notice these types of things—had tipped her off.

Once again she'd forced herself to drive sedately by as the most hideous type of danger surrounded her.

Then they'd left town. It didn't matter if Melissa might call or not, they couldn't stay in Kansas City.

She drove west, since it was in the opposite direction from the Northeast, where the Organization's main office was located. Or, at least the main office where they showed their *public* face.

It wouldn't have mattered which direction she drove. The days wore on her. Lack of finances wore on her.

Why were baby formula and diapers so damn expensive?

Even only eating one meal a day herself and spending every night they possibly could in the car, she was still down to her last twenty dollars just outside Denver.

Desperate, she'd taken to shoplifting the stuff she could for the babies, using all her spare cash for gas, and had been successful a few times.

But it looked like her luck had run out today here in the tiny town of Risk Peak.

At least she wasn't in jail waiting for someone from the Organization to come kill her—or worse, take her back into captivity with them—so maybe her luck wasn't completely gone.

Not that the screaming in the back seat was any indication of that. Bree gripped the steering wheel tighter, feeling pressure sitting like a hundred-pound weight on her chest. Breathing was becoming harder.

She tried to think rationally. She couldn't go any farther right now. Christian and Beth were hungry and needed to be changed. And she couldn't drive in this condition. She was too strung out, her body crashing now that the adrenaline wasn't coursing through her system.

When she saw the diner the cop had mentioned, she pulled in. Might as well take him up on his offer of a free meal. For the past week she'd been living off a loaf of bread, a jar of peanut butter and what food she could steal from sneaking into the lobbies of hotels that offered free breakfasts.

God, she was so tired. When was the last time she got more than two hours of sleep in a row? Maybe food would help. It couldn't possibly hurt.

She grabbed the diaper bag filled with the shoplifted formula packets. If she'd known someone was going to buy her formula, she would've gotten the cans of the powder. Those were so much more economical.

Bree was now an expert on finding the cheapest possible formula.

She got out and hefted Beth in her carrier up with one arm, then walked around to get Christian with the other. She only made it a couple of steps before she had to stop, dizziness assailing her. She took deep breaths, trying to force strength into her limbs. She could not pass out here, leaving the babies defenseless. The door got more blurry as she moved toward it, but she forced herself to take the steps. She just needed to get inside and sit down. Then she would be okay.

She had to be okay. She didn't have any other option.

The bell that clanked against the door as she opened it seemed almost at a distance. Bree walked as straight as she could, trying not to stumble, toward the first booth she saw.

She almost cried in relief when she put the carriers down on the booth with a thump. Neither twin liked being set down so hard, and they began crying harder.

"Shh, it's okay," she whispered, the words sounding garbled to her own ears.

She half sat, half fell into the booth next to one of the babies. At this point she couldn't even tell which one it was.

"Good thing one of you is a boy and one is a girl, or I would never know who was who," she whispered.

They both just kept screaming.

For the life of her, Bree couldn't remember how to get them to stop crying. She just wished everything would stop spinning before she got sick.

When an older lady wearing a bright yellow apron walked up to the table, Bree wondered if they were going to get kicked out. And what in the world she was going to do if they did.

"Can I help you, sweetie?" the woman said.

Bree just stared at the woman for a few moments. "I never planned on being a mother. This is too hard. I was the wrong choice."

She was saying too much, maybe putting them all in danger. But the older woman just smiled and sat down across from Bree. "I think all mothers feel like that sometimes. How about if I help you? It looks like these little guys need to be fed."

Bree tried to study the woman's face, but it was going in and out of focus. "Yes, they need their bottle. I need to give them their bottle."

"When was the last time you got a decent night's sleep, honey?"

Hadn't she just been asking herself that question?

"When I was ten." Before she'd realized what the Organization really was capable of.

The older woman chuckled and patted Bree's hand. She wasn't used to touch, but this felt warm, comforting. "I'm sure it feels like it. I'm Cheryl Andrews. Me and my husband, Dan, own the Sunrise Diner. We raised three kids of our own, so if you don't mind, I'd like to help you out and make a bottle for your little ones. Give you a chance to rest."

Could she trust this woman?

Did she have a choice?

"Why don't you just let me get the bottles ready for you. Is it okay if I go into the diaper bag?"

Bree just nodded, everything still fuzzy as she watched the woman walk. Bree was still staring at the doorway when the woman came back out a few moments later, an older man behind her.

She'd made the bottles.

"Thank you," she whispered. She felt like crying she was so thankful for the kindness.

"This is my Dan. He and I are just going to feed your babies. Is that okay? You just sit there and rest, okay?"

"Okay." She leaned her head against the back of the booth and watched as the older couple spoke soothingly to both children before putting the bottles up to their tiny faces.

Then there was blessed silence.

Then there was nothing at all.

THE FIRST THING that penetrated Bree's consciousness as she awoke was the silence. Followed by liquid under her cheek. It took her a moment to realize she'd been sleeping with her arms folded on a table.

Where were Christian and Beth?

She jackknifed upright, looking around. The carriers were still in the booth, but neither baby was there.

Terror slammed into her like a sledgehammer. How long had she been asleep? How could she have let this happen? She bolted out of the booth, looking around frantically, then came to an abrupt halt.

There at a corner table, the old couple—what were their names? Dan and Sherri? No, Cheryl—were holding the babies, cooing and smiling at them.

A half dozen other people of varying ages were standing around, too, talking, smiling, reaching over Dan and Cheryl to make funny faces at the twins.

It was like something out of a television show. Not even a show from this decade. Something from forty years ago.

It definitely wasn't something she'd ever been a part of herself. Emotions weren't easy for her on any given day. But this? She had no idea how to react to this scenario.

"Hey, honey." Cheryl smiled up at her, a noncrying Christian in her arms. "Are you feeling better? We weren't sure if you needed a doctor but finally figured maybe you just needed a little break from these two. Babies can be so exhausting."

"Um, yes. I guess I did."

Dan smiled at her, standing and handing Beth over. "Thanks for letting us hold your young'uns." His Southern accent was more pronounced than Cheryl's. "We haven't had babies to hold in a long time. Hope you don't mind."

Bree just shook her head, still feeling like she was in some black-and-white television show. As if someone would tell John Boy good-night at any moment.

"No, I don't mind. Thank you. I'm not sure what happened, but I feel a lot better."

Dan patted her shoulder. "Why don't you sit down with everyone and I'll go make you something to eat in the back."

Bree looked at the group, teeth grinding. She didn't have anything against people sitting around chatting, she just didn't think she was capable of joining them. Didn't know *how*.

Dan smiled gently at her. "Or, if gabbing like a bunch of squawking ducks doesn't suit your fancy, you're welcome to come in the back with me. Bring the baby, or I'm positive they'll all fight to the death for the chance to hold her."

Bree wasn't quite sure what to do, so she kept Beth in her arms as she followed Dan into the kitchen, using the baby almost as a shield. Not that she thought the older man would do her any physical harm, but from all the questions she knew would have to be coming.

But the only question Dan asked was if she would prefer the breakfast sampler or Cheryl's famous meat loaf.

Bree would much rather have the breakfast food, but she didn't want to make a social faux pas by insulting the famous meat loaf in this sitcom she was currently starring in.

"The breakfast sampler does come with pancakes, so I can't blame you if that's the route you'd rather go." Dan winked at her.

"I do like pancakes," she whispered, pulling Beth a little closer.

"Then pancakes it is."

She offered to help, but Dan would hear nothing of it as he made her food. When Cheryl stuck her head through the window and told him someone wanted the daily, Dan didn't even bat an eye, just immediately started fixing the meat loaf platter.

He never asked Bree any questions about where she was from, what she was doing or why she'd fallen asleep in the middle of his restaurant. Just whistled, working contentedly in a kitchen he obviously was very familiar with. He passed the daily special order out to Cheryl, then added a couple more pancakes to the griddle, putting them on Bree's plate as soon as she'd finished the first ones.

"Oh, I don't know if I should…" She trailed off. It wasn't that she wasn't hungry enough to eat them, she just didn't want to be completely greedy.

"Might as well finish them now," he said. "I hate to waste food if I don't need to."

That was all the invitation she needed. He even reached out and took Beth from her so she could more easily cut and engulf the pancakes.

She took Beth back when she was finished. She was

pretty amazed how a couple hours of sleep and a full meal made her almost feel like she could handle the situation she found herself in.

Although that was just as much fiction as any sitcom. Except not as funny.

Because what was she going to do once she left here?

"Thank you." She took the plate back to the dishwashing sink and began washing it off.

"It's my pleasure. I enjoy seeing someone partaking in my food with such exuberance—"

Cheryl came rushing back through the kitchen door, Christian sleeping in one carrier, the empty one in her other hand. "We just had a bus full of tourists pull up. I sent Judy home an hour ago because her husband's been so sick. I didn't think we'd have much business tonight."

Dan began setting out items of food he'd need for the group. "By the time you call her and she gets back here, it'll be too late."

"I can help." The words were out of her mouth before Bree knew they would come—a common problem for her—but it was still true. It was the least she could do given that they'd basically allowed her to set up camp here. Tanner had told her to put it on his tab, but there was no way she was doing that. "The kids have been fed, and if you've got an office or somewhere we can sit them, I'll keep an eye on them while I wait or bus tables or whatever you need. Consider it payment for today's room and board."

Both Dan and Cheryl were shaking their heads no, communicating silently with each other, and she thought they weren't going to let her. She didn't blame them—they didn't know her at all. But Cheryl opened the door off the back of the kitchen to a small office. “If you don’t mind, we can definitely use your help. Dan and I are getting too old for rushes like this alone. But you’re definitely going to get paid. That’s not negotiable.”

“I sort of lost my purse. I don’t really have stuff for tax purposes.” She didn’t like lying to them, but the less they knew about her, the better.

Dan tossed her an apron. “We’ll worry about Uncle Sam later. Right now, get those young’uns stashed away and let’s get these tourists fed.”

Chapter Four

Eight days after watching Bree drive away, Tanner walked from the department's office over to the Sunrise Diner. His body nearly dragged with exhaustion. He wanted a good meal and fifteen hours of sleep in his own bed, as soon as possible.

He'd spent the last eight days working almost nonstop on an interstate task force a couple hours away, in a town only slightly larger than Risk Peak, combating a rising gang problem plaguing Colorado more and more. Tanner didn't mind helping out, even though he'd never be able to put in for all the overtime hours he'd worked.

The way he saw it, stopping these types of criminal situations before they made it to Risk Peak was worth the extra hours.

And the hours had been hell. As he and his fellow law enforcement officers had moved in for arrests after days and multiple sleepless nights of undercover work and observation, one of the suspects had grabbed a preteen boy—skinny and terrified—as a human shield. Before Tanner could even talk the perp down, he'd stabbed the kid and run.

They'd caught the guy, but someone way too young and completely innocent had paid the price.

The overall outcome had been heralded a success. The gang had been broken up before it could take root in the community. But none of the men and women working the case had felt like celebrating. They'd driven out a criminal element, but not in time to save the life of that one boy.

Tanner knew it could happen in any town at any time. He was willing to volunteer hours to keep the front lines away from Risk Peak. Because if he didn't fight it when he could, it might end up being some kid from here in the morgue.

He walked down the streets he'd been walking his whole life. These people were his to protect, and he took that very seriously, just like his father had.

He was looking forward to a meal with friendly faces and people dropping by his table just to say hello. Today he would not be taking for granted that there was always tomorrow to chat.

But inside the Sunrise, everybody seemed too busy to pay him much attention. The diner wasn't particularly full even though it was nearly dinner, but everyone seemed preoccupied.

A couple of people gave him a little wave, but nobody came over to talk to him. He rubbed his fingers against his tired eyes, then down his cheeks that definitely needed a shave again. He was being too sensitive. Exhaustion could blow a lot of things out of proportion.

But why the hell were five people huddled around the back corner booth—including Mrs. Andrews? He couldn't recall her sitting down during a dinner shift his entire life.

Judy Marshall, who'd gone to school with Tanner's younger sister, brought his normal cup of coffee over to his table. "Haven't seen you around for a while."

"Yeah, I've been working over in Pueblo County helping out with a gang issue. I'm ready to sleep for a week. I'll just have whatever's on special."

"Sounds good. I'll get Mr. A started on it for you."

"Is Mrs. A feeling all right? Why is she sitting in the booth rather than working? That's not like her."

Judy rolled her eyes. "She finally found something she loves more than Mr. Andrews and the Sunrise. Not that I can blame her."

Tanner raised an eyebrow. The older woman might have found someone she loved more than her husband, but more than this diner? No way.

Whatever was causing the commotion over in the corner, it definitely had everyone's attention. He was too tired to worry about it. Nobody was hurt or breaking the law, so he was just going to sit and enjoy his meal and get home.

That resolution lasted about two minutes.

He grabbed his coffee and started making his way toward the corner booth, to see for himself what the fuss was about. He wasn't quite there when he heard a baby's muffled cry. That would explain it.

And it immediately made him think of Bree. She hadn't been far from his mind all week. Was she all right? Had she and the babies made it safely to wherever they were going?

The chances of him ever knowing were slim to none.

He caught Mrs. A's gaze and gave her a little salute with his coffee cup. Then the woman uncharacteristically shifted her eyes to the side and down. If Tanner had been interrogating a suspect, he would've taken it as an indication that the perp was hiding something. Acting suspiciously.

Exhaustion was definitely clouding his judgment. The Andrewses were as straightforward and honest as people came. And Mrs. Andrews wasn't someone who hid her actions from anyone. Other people's opinions had never concerned her.

He shrugged it off and was turning back to the table when a second cry joined the first. Even louder.

That set of pipes Tanner recognized. He immediately spun back toward the booth, marching all the way to the edge. Sure enough, there they were. Twins.

He didn't know a lot about babies, but he was willing to bet these were Bree's. He looked around but didn't see her anywhere.

He crossed his arms over his chest. "What's going on, Mrs. A?"

The older woman raised a single eyebrow. "I've got a couple of infants here crying. It happens. You cried quite a bit too when you were this age, if I recall."

Tanner just studied her. Overfamiliarity was an issue from time to time, since he'd known most of the people in Risk Peak his entire life. Generally, Tanner used it to his advantage.

But today it wasn't going to be so easy.

"I have no problem with babies crying," he finally answered evenly. "I'm fairly certain they're not doing anything against the law. Where is their mother?"

Because she, he wasn't so certain about.

"To be honest, I'm not entirely sure right at this moment." Mrs. A shifted the baby in her arms and wiggled a pacifier in its mouth until it latched on and stopped crying. Across from her, Glenda Manning, who had a couple of teenage children of her own, cooed at the baby she was bouncing.

"Whose children are these, Cheryl?" He didn't take the use of her first name lightly.

Neither did she. "Why do you care, *Tanner*?"

One of the women sitting across from Mrs. Andrews looked like she might speak up, but was given the stink eye so quickly she abruptly looked away.

Why would Mrs. A be making such a big deal out of this if Bree wasn't in more trouble? Why wouldn't the older woman just say they were holding the babies while the mom was in the bathroom or at the gas station or wherever she was? Tanner would've believed that with no suspicion at all. The fact that Mrs. A refused to give any information was what made it suspicious.

A husky feminine voice spoke behind him. "I'm through for the day, Cheryl. Thank you again so much for watch—"

Tanner spun around to see the woman who hadn't been far out of his thoughts since he'd watched her drive away over a week ago. His breath almost whistled through his teeth. She was definitely as beautiful as he remembered. The long brown hair falling around her shoulders made him want to reach out and touch it to see if it was as soft as it was in his dreams.

"You." Her big green eyes widened, and the small

smile faded from her face. Tension instantly ratcheted through her slim body.

He tilted his head to the side and raised an eyebrow. "Me."

"You two know each other?" Mrs. Andrews asked.

Tanner nodded then looked back at Bree. "We met at the drugstore a few days ago, although I don't think you got my name. Tanner Dempsey."

"Bree," she whispered.

"I remember. I was under the impression that you were in a hurry to get out of Risk Peak."

"I, um…" She looked over at Mrs. A. "I, um…"

Mrs. Andrews stood with the now-quiet baby and walked over to stand beside her. "Bree was kind enough to come work for Dan and me. We needed some help around here."

There was definitely more to this story than was being given, evidenced by the silence surrounding them. But no one seemed to want to provide any details.

"Tanner, got your dinner here," Judy called out from behind him. "Mr. Andrews made country-fried steak just for you."

The Andrewses never let anyone forget that they'd lived in Georgia before moving to Colorado. This was probably the only place in the whole state where you could find genuine Southern cooking.

Tanner studied the two women in front of him. Bree was reaching over to get the baby Mrs. Andrews was holding. This one was in pink.

"Thanks for watching them, Mrs. Andrews," she whispered before kissing the child's fuzzy head.

"Call me, Cheryl, sweetheart. We've already talked about that."

He crossed his arms over his chest. "Why does she get to call you Cheryl and I have to call you Mrs. Andrews?"

She narrowed her eyes at him. "Because I haven't known her since she was in diapers. And I didn't have to take her out of a Sunday School class one time and swat her butt because she put a frog down Linda Dugas's dress."

Tanner chuckled with everyone else. It wasn't the only time he'd been dragged out of Sunday School class.

And he was smart enough to know when a battle wasn't going to be won head-on. He gave them both a nod. "Fine. I'll go eat. There will be plenty of time to talk later."

Because he sure as hell wasn't going anywhere. The exhaustion that had plagued him was gone. He ate his food, watching Bree pack up the babies and get ready to leave. The other women tried to get her to sit down and talk, but she didn't seem interested. And she was very careful not to look over in his direction.

This woman had *trouble* written all over her. Whether she was chasing it or it was chasing her remained to be seen.

He grabbed Judy as she drifted by with a coffee cup, watching Bree walk out the door without once looking his way. "Is the new girl with the babies staying at one of the hotels?"

Judy looked uncomfortable. "Actually, I'm not exactly sure where Bree is staying."

"It's okay, Judy. I'll talk to the *officer*." Mrs. Andrews put her hand on Judy's shoulder before sitting down across from Tanner.

Tanner took another bite of his steak. "You going to threaten to snatch me out of Sunday School again? My mom might be a little shocked to get the call."

"I just don't want Judy stuck in the middle of anything. You seem pretty interested in our new employee."

"My interest became piqued because you were dodging my questions." He chewed his food. "That's not something I've ever known you to do."

Mrs. Andrews let out a little sigh. "That girl wandered in here last week half a minute from a complete breakdown. She needed help, so we offered her a job. Nothing wrong with that."

Tanner took a sip of his coffee. "No, nothing wrong with that. Did she mention she and I met last week also, probably right before she came over here?"

This was obviously news to Mrs. A. The older woman bent her head to study her nails. "No, she didn't."

"I caught her shoplifting. Stuff for the babies, but Bree very definitely had no plans—and probably no means—of paying for it."

Mrs. A straightened in her seat, eyes narrowing. "Well, you just tell me how much it was and Dan and I will pay for it ourselves. I'll go over and talk to Gary, and we can get it worked out."

"There's no need. It was handled before she even got out of the store. So technically, no laws were broken. But the point is, she's *trouble*. I'm not sure what kind yet, but I know we don't have all the facts when it comes to that woman. Has she told you anything about herself?"

"No. She keeps quiet. Does any work we ask her to and either keeps the babies with her or lets us hold them out front. She's got quite a fan club now. Everybody wants to hold them. But Bree never really talks much to anyone."

All Tanner's exhaustion was back. He rubbed a hand over his eyes. "And none of this seems unusual to you?"

"She's not a bad person, Tanner."

He gritted his teeth. "Let's not forget that my father once felt that way about someone. That kid seemed young and innocent and helpless, too. Ended up costing Dad his life."

Mrs. Andrews reached out and took his hand on the table. "It's not the same. That gang situation was trouble from the first moment he got involved. The people were bad seeds. That's not what this is."

Wasn't it? Not gang related, but definitely trouble.

"No offense, but we don't know what this is. Maybe Bree isn't a criminal outside of an occasional shoplifting charge—"

"She did that because she was desperate!"

Tanner let out a sigh. "Fine, let's say I agree with you, which I actually do. Let's say she's not a criminal, only desperate. Desperate people do some pretty dangerous stuff, too. It's my responsibility to look out for the well-being of the town."

"So what do you want us to do? Just kick her out? Send her on her way?"

"How about if you just give me her full name and Social Security number from her tax stuff, and I'll run her through the system. See if anything comes up. At least that way we'll know."

"I'm afraid we can't do that."

Tanner raised an eyebrow. "Can't or won't?"

Mrs. Andrews let out a sigh. "Can't."

He muttered a curse under his breath. "You're paying her under the table."

Her lips tightened. "We are allotted a certain amount of labor wages every year without having to claim it on our taxes."

He rubbed a hand across his face. "I'm not going to turn you into the IRS, Mrs. A. I'm concerned for your *safety*. You don't even know this woman's Social Security number."

"Actually, we don't even know her last name. She didn't want to give it, so we just let it go."

Tanner swallowed a curse that would definitely get him snatched out of the Sunday School class. "I can't just let it go."

She nodded. "I understand, but she's not the bad guy."

Tanner thought of those big green eyes and the exhaustion and desperation that seemed to hang over her like a cloud even now. "Maybe not. But I'd still like to talk to her further. Which hotel is she staying at?"

"Neither. She's staying at the apartment just outside town Dan and I spruced up last year for when the kids come to visit. We're letting her have it for free for right now, until she gets back on her feet. And don't you try to talk us out of it, Tanner Dempsey. Both Dan and I agree it's the right thing to do."

He took the last sip of his coffee. "I'm not going to

try to talk you out of it. But I'm not going to ignore that she could be a threat to this town. That woman has secrets, and I intend to find out what they are."

Chapter Five

Bree waited for the knock at her door she'd known would be coming from the moment she saw Tanner Dempsey in the diner. She'd done her best to avoid eye contact with the sexy officer but had no doubt he'd be showing up here soon.

He wanted answers. And he didn't strike her as someone who would stop until he got them.

Should she run? Try to get out before he arrived?

She looked around the small one-bedroom apartment that Dan and Cheryl were letting them stay at as part of her "salary." The last eight nights had been the closest Bree had come to a full night's sleep in the six weeks since her life had been thrown into total upheaval with the care of the twins.

Those babies were a piece of her now. She would do anything to protect them, even what was almost impossible for her: trusting other people.

She didn't know exactly why the Andrewses were helping her, just knew right now she didn't have any other options, so she would accept it. She had a door that locked, a general feeling of security and their basic needs were being met.

Maybe she wasn't exactly doing a great job with the twins' care—Christian still cried all the time, obviously subconsciously aware in his little baby brain that Bree wasn't a qualified caretaker—but hopefully if Melissa could see them now she wouldn't completely regret her decision to trust Bree.

And being safe here had allowed Bree to start looking into the data on the hard drive Melissa had sent with the twins.

Very, very carefully.

The data on it could only be accessed by pinging off the Organization's own servers. Bree was an expert at covering her tracks, but nobody could completely hide from them while simultaneously attempting to access their own network. The best she could do was make them think she was harmless.

And that she definitely wasn't Bethany Malone, the hacker genius they'd helped create, forging her in brutality.

But coming at the data this way was slow, especially when Bree wasn't sure what exactly she was accessing and how it might help Melissa. She just knew she had to take some time to try while she was relatively safe, even if it meant working for hours at night after already putting in long shifts during the day.

Christian began to cry, so she picked him up, walking back and forth while rubbing his back. "Come on now, kiddo. I've had a full day on my feet. How about if you settle down so I can worry myself sick before the big bad cop arrives."

Beth, unlike her cranky brother, stayed asleep, as she tended to do. Even when she was awake, she was all smiles and big eyes. But both of them were growing more every day. Staying awake a little longer. Showing just a little more personality.

Soon they wouldn't be content to stay in their carriers most of the time. They'd want to sit up and look around more. Not long after that, they'd begin crawling.

That was beyond scary to think about.

"I know your mama misses you, buddy. She wouldn't believe how big you've gotten in the weeks since she's seen you. I'm going to try to get you back to her real soon."

As if those were the words Christian had been waiting to hear, he snuggled into her shoulder and closed his eyes.

Bree had only known these beautiful babies for a few weeks, and she already knew it was going to tear a hole in her when she had to give them back to Melissa.

But that was stupid. Bree had been completely alone for the past three years since her mom died, and really even before that, when her mom had started to deteriorate. She was used to being alone. *Loved* being alone. A few weeks couldn't change her entire outlook on life.

But she was already afraid it had.

The knock she'd been expecting finally came. Now she was about to find out whether the choice to stay here was taken out of her hands. She opened the door.

"Officer." She gave a nod of greeting.

"Looks like you were expecting me."

God, he was still as sexy as she'd remembered. Half a foot taller than her with thick black hair and warm brown eyes, before she quickly looked away from them.

He was dressed in jeans and a beige Henley that molded over his chest.

Studying his shoulders and biceps, Bree let herself imagine what it would be like to be in the arms of a man. Not any man, *this* man. Being on the run most of her life hadn't left time for any sort of relationships. Not friendships and definitely not romantic entanglements. She'd never wanted to.

But, now…

She finally looked up and found him staring down at her. He was waiting for her to speak. "Um, yeah, I realized you would probably have some questions about why I was still in town."

He gave a nod. "Can I come in?"

"If I say no, are you going to arrest me?"

"Have you done anything for me to arrest you for?" One dark brow raised.

"Not today." She meant it as a joke, but he was obviously taking her seriously.

"Then I guess I won't be arresting you today. And if you tell me I can't come in then I'll leave. But I'll take Mrs. A's lemon pie with me." He held up a paper bag.

Her mouth immediately watered. "That's not fair, it's my favorite. How did you know?"

"You're breathing, aren't you? Of course it's your favorite. It's everybody's favorite. If it wasn't your favorite then I *would* have to arrest you."

She gestured for him to enter. "Since you have pie."

"I also have a chicken sandwich from Mrs. A. She said you left without getting your normal meal and that you weren't allowed to have the pie until you ate it."

She took the bag and turned back toward the small

kitchen table in the corner. He followed her in, closing the door behind him.

"Cheryl says I don't eat enough." Bree put the chicken sandwich on a plate. "She makes me eat at least one meal at the diner every day."

He chuckled, a casually confident sound that mesmerized her. Bree couldn't remember ever chuckling like that in her life. And if she had, it definitely wouldn't have sounded that sexy.

"Mrs. Andrews says *everyone* doesn't eat enough. I would find it less suspicious if she wasn't the owner of a restaurant. But in your case, I think she might be right. Between being a new mother and working every day, you're probably burning a lot of calories."

"Do you want any of this sandwich?" She gestured for him to sit with her, but he shook his head.

"No, thanks. I already ate plenty."

She nodded. "So, Dempsey. Is that the same Dempsey as the teenager that comes in a couple times a week to help out at the diner?"

"That would probably be my cousin Robbie. My father's brother's son. I've got a lot of family that lives around here. How about you, got any family?"

She took another bite of her chicken sandwich. "None here in Risk Peak."

He leaned against the wall, stretching his long legs out in front of him. "Oh, I'm damn sure I would know it if you lived around here, believe me. Got any family anywhere else?"

She took another bite of chicken and chewed it slowly, more to give her time to decide what to say. She had a driver's license that said Bree Daniels. If he checked that out, it wouldn't bring the whole world crashing down. So she was probably best off sticking with it.

"No, no family. Just me."

He tilted his head to the side, eyes narrowing. "And the babies."

"Of course." Damn it. She was so used to thinking of herself as alone. "Christian and Beth."

"And their father? He's family, too, in a way. He around anywhere?"

She stuffed more food in her mouth. "He's not in the picture."

She didn't know if the twins' father was friend or foe. There were so many things she needed to ask Melissa. Every day she waited for that phone to ring, but it never did.

He let her finish eating without any more questions, but she didn't deceive herself into thinking he was done. She immediately unwrapped the pie when she finished her sandwich. Partially to hold off more questions, but she hadn't been lying when she said it was her favorite.

"It looks like Cheryl put two slices in here. Do you want one?"

He nodded and sat down with her at the table. She got him a fork, and they both began to eat. She was only on her third bite when she looked over and found him finishing his.

"That's good pie," he said, shoveling the last bite into his mouth.

Bree watched with wide eyes, scooting her plate closer to her protectively. "You're not one for savoring, are you?"

He leaned back in his chair and smiled.

Good God, that smile was lethal.

She sat frozen as he reached across the table and wiped a little piece of pie that had gotten caught on the corner of her mouth.

He brought the crumb up to his lips and licked it off. "Oh, I'm definitely for savoring when the time is right. For savoring every little bit as long as possible."

She had the distinct feeling they weren't talking about pie anymore.

But then he straightened in his chair, breaking the spell. "But when it comes to one of the Sunrise lemon pies, I had two siblings and a mother and father all vying for as much of one pie as possible every Saturday evening when I was growing up. Whoever finished first generally got to eat whatever bits had been left in the tray. I learned how to eat my slice in three bites when it counted."

She put another bite in her mouth and chewed slowly. Except for the meals she'd eaten at the Sunrise Diner over the last week, she'd never really eaten with anyone else. Even her mother hadn't been interested in family meals at the table. She'd been too paranoid.

"Wow." She took another bite quickly, not completely sure he wouldn't try to make a grab for hers. "I guess you can buy your own pie now."

"Yeah, but sometimes my brother, sister and I still take a turn at it when we're together for a meal. My mom gets in on the action, too."

She could almost imagine it. A table full of grown people eating the delicious dessert as fast as they could to fight for leftovers.

It seemed…nice.

"Did your dad wise up? Does he stay out of the fray now?"

She peeked over at Tanner just in time to see the smile completely fade from his face. "No. My dad's dead."

She threw her gaze down to her pie again. "Oh. I'm sorry for your loss."

Mentioning his dad had completely broken the mood. Tanner stiffened in his chair. "What kind of trouble are you in, Bree?"

"What makes you think I'm in any trouble at all?"

"You've got *trouble* all but tattooed on your forehead. It was one thing when you were just passing through. But now you've stuck around, so whatever trouble you're in becomes my problem, too. I don't want to see the Andrewses get hurt."

"I'm not going to hurt them. I'm not going to hurt anyone." She just needed to stay under the radar.

He ran his fingers through that thick dark hair. "The babies' dad… Did he hurt you, maybe? I can help if that's the case."

She shook her head. "No, it's nothing like that."

"Are you in trouble with the law? On the run? You may not believe me, but I can help with that, too. Almost always, things go more leniently with a judge when a person turns herself in of her own accord."

She let out a sigh. "I'm not wanted by the law, either. I just…needed some changes in my life. Then before I knew it, I was broke, but the babies still needed all their baby stuff."

That was as close to the truth as she could come

without bringing down the type of danger even the police weren't equipped to deal with.

Tanner studied her with those deep brown eyes that missed nothing. She forced herself to meet his gaze, to remain calm.

To not act guilty.

"So, if you told me your last name, and I run it right now in our system, there's not going to be some husband who has reported a kidnapping of his children by his wife? There's not going to be an APB out for your arrest somewhere?"

She stood and walked over to the diaper bag and got out her driver's license. She walked back to him and handed over the license. "Bree Daniels."

She'd surprised him. He'd thought she was just going to tell him a name. A lie.

But he recovered quickly. "You won't mind if I call this in and have them run it real quickly at the office?"

She crossed her arms over her chest. "Not at all."

He stood and pulled out his phone, an old flip version like the one she had. That reassured her. The Organization couldn't steal the info from that phone. Although if they figured out she was here, there weren't many places to hide in a town this size.

Tanner turned away from her to talk to someone in his office, reading her name and driver's license number.

Bree Daniels would look real in any system. She had a Social Security number, work history, even had a library card if someone searched that far.

Bree had built the identity herself after her mother

died. Had thought she would use this identity for a much longer time. Had hoped to be Bree Daniels forever.

That might not be possible soon.

He hung up and sat back down at the table with her. "They'll call me back in a few minutes. Shouldn't take long."

She stood and began clearing the dishes off the table. "So you're from Missouri. Were the babies born in Kansas City?"

Damn it. She hadn't thought about Beth and Christian. Would he try to track down more information about them from hospitals? How many twins could possibly have been born there in the last few months?

She rinsed the plate off in the sink. "No, I was actually out of town when they were born."

When she turned, she found him studying her. "Were they premature?"

The more information she gave, the more easily she could get caught in a lie. "Not by much, a little early, I guess. Not unusual with twins."

He was still studying her too closely. "You look like you're in amazing shape."

She turned to wipe down the counter.

Keep calm.

He didn't know anything. He was fishing.

After she finished wiping, she turned and gave him the biggest smile she could muster. "Well, Mrs. Andrews's lemon pie certainly is not helping."

He was going to push the issue, she could tell. But his phone buzzed in his hand. He kept his eyes pinned on her as he lifted it to his ear.

He listened to the report without saying much of

anything. At the end, he thanked whoever was on the line and hung up. He stood.

"It seems I owe you an apology. Bree Daniels has no APBs out for her arrest, and no one has reported you either as a missing person or as someone of interest in any cases."

"Glad to hear it."

He wanted to say more. She could tell he wanted to say so much more, but one of the babies started to fuss from over in the playpen where they slept.

Tanner nodded. "You've had a full day of work, and I'm sure those kiddos don't sleep very long. I'll get out of your hair."

She was surprised at the disappointment that washed over her. She wanted him gone, right? She didn't long for a normal conversation with him, because that wasn't very smart.

Smart is how you stay alive.

"Thank you for bringing dinner," she whispered.

He nodded then walked to the door and opened it, looking back at her. "Bree?"

"Yes?"

Those brown eyes pinned her. "I'll see you around. *Soon.*"

It was both a threat and a promise.

Chapter Six

When Bree's name had come back clean in the report, Tanner immediately went to the station and ran it again himself.

It had been clean again.

After going home and sleeping for twelve hours, he'd come back to the station and run it again.

And yet again, *nothing.*

Bree Daniels was a law-abiding citizen with no criminal record and nothing to make anyone wary. Everything about her seemed legitimate. She was twenty-four years old, a little younger than he would've thought, but being a mother of two probably made someone grow up quickly. She'd never been married and, as she'd said, had no run-ins with the law, barring the shoplifting incident.

There was no reason to think she was anything other than what she said she was: someone making changes in her life that hadn't worked out the way she thought they would.

But Tanner couldn't shake the feeling that there was a lot more trouble surrounding her than that. Every instinct he had—honed by his ten years of law enforcement—told him there was more to Bree Daniels than met the eye.

A battle waged inside him between his sworn duty to protect Risk Peak and all of Grand County, and this unfamiliar need to help Bree with whatever danger was at her heels.

Because no clean record was going to convince him that she wasn't frightened of *something.*

So here he was a week later, having his second cup of coffee at the Sunrise, just like the last seven mornings. Mr. and Mrs. Andrews had taken to just ignoring him, since they knew he was there in a half-official capacity. In the unspoken battle between team Bree and team Tanner, they'd obviously chosen her side.

Tanner wasn't surprised. It was hard for anyone not to be protective of the quiet woman. Not to mention Bree could've been Jack the Ripper and the Andrewses would've loved her because of the babies.

Tanner sipped and watched the woman in question. One thing was for sure: she was becoming *more* fragile, not less so. In the week since he'd talked to her at her apartment, she'd lost weight, despite Mrs. Andrews's insistence that she eat, and the circles under her eyes had become more pronounced. Maybe the babies kept her up all night. It couldn't be easy having infant twins, even though they seemed pretty manageable during the day.

Mrs. A walked up beside him and refilled his coffee cup, both of them watching Bree clear off the table that had just been vacated.

"You're worried about her," she said.

Tanner turned slightly toward the older woman but

kept his attention on Bree. "I thought you weren't talking to me."

Mrs. A shrugged. "Only if you're going to spend your time trying to convince me Bree is dangerous. You watch her like she's a suspect."

"It's my job to keep the people of Risk Peak safe."

And while he couldn't deny his attraction to Bree, he definitely didn't trust her.

Mrs. Andrews's lips tightened. "I'll be sure to let you know if she, or her two obviously trained miniature assassins, show any sign of evildoings."

Mrs. A was about to revert to the silent treatment. Tanner touched her arm. "Bree looks more tired, don't you think?"

She let out a sigh. "Like the weight of the world is on her shoulders."

"Is that normal for a new mother, do you think? Maybe it's postpartum depression or something. Or maybe the babies don't let her get sleep at night."

"Well, she's going to get sleep tonight. I already told her Dan and I are going to keep those babies so she could get a full night's rest."

"She agreed to that?"

Mrs. Andrews nodded. "Shows you how desperate she is, doesn't it? But I told her how the whole world would look different if she just got some good sleep." She shrugged. "Then I threatened to fire her if she didn't take us up on the offer, although I don't think she believed me."

Mrs. A left, and Tanner continued to observe Bree from his stool. She studiously ignored him, sweeping up the restaurant, pausing every once in a while to kiss or coo at the babies, who sat with Mr. Andrews and some of the couple's friends who were stopping by more often.

Having adorable twin babies that needed to be cuddled was good for diner business.

And Bree was a hard worker. Nobody minded helping her, since she was working so hard.

And just like that, he was back to that battle within himself again. On one hand, she was exactly what she seemed to be: a down-on-her-luck single mother.

On the other hand…

What the hell was up with that piece-of-junk flip phone of hers? He had one because that was the choice the department had made concerning official phones. No smartphones.

But why would Bree have one so basic? Hers looked like it would barely even call or text. He'd never seen her use it even once, but she always wanted it in her possession. He'd seen panic fall over her features a couple of days ago when she realized she'd left it in the back. She'd rushed to the kitchen and came back out clutching it to her.

It was like she was waiting for a call that never came.

But from whom? And about what? Was that what was causing her to look more weary and fragile with each passing day?

Or was that all in Tanner's head?

All his colleagues at the sheriff's office teased him about how much time he spent studying Bree. He took the good-natured ribbing with a smile. They thought he had a crush on her and joked about him being obsessed.

They weren't wrong.

But he couldn't let it go.

Tanner took his last sip of coffee, put some money on the counter and left. He wasn't surprised when Bree didn't acknowledge him.

What was he expecting? That she would run over to him and spill all the secrets she was keeping?

Tanner needed to pull his head out of his ass. The sheriff had entrusted him and made him the captain of the entire southeastern section of Grand County three years ago. There was a whole office full of people who looked up to and expected leadership from him.

So he damn well better start acting like the seasoned law enforcement agent he was, rather than a high schooler with a crush.

He headed to the office and found the rest of his day taken up with the mundane tasks of keeping his section of the county running smoothly.

But Bree was never far from his mind.

Later that night when Ronnie Kitchens, one of Tanner's deputies, called in sick, Tanner agreed to take his shift even though it meant working a double. Anything was better than sitting at home with his own thoughts, knowing Bree was alone in her little apartment tonight.

His thoughts about her were inappropriate enough without the temptation of potentially acting on them. Focusing on work was much better.

He was out doing a normal town drive-through, proud of himself for keeping well away from Bree's apartment, when he glanced over at the library parking lot as he drove past.

Then did an immediate double take, letting out a string of curses inside his Bronco.

What the hell was Bree's car doing in the small, secluded parking lot of the Risk Peak's library?

His immediate inclination was to swerve in there and confront her, but he forced himself to keep driving so she wouldn't notice him. His Bronco was an official vehicle, but unmarked. Anybody around town would know it was him immediately, but maybe not her.

Was she meeting someone?

He circled around the back of the library, turning off his lights and killing the engine in the grocery store parking lot across the street. She wouldn't spot him unless she turned around and really looked.

He grabbed the binoculars in the back seat and looked through them to get a better view. It was definitely Bree in the car, and no one was with her.

Yet.

She was working on a laptop. Why the hell would she be sitting in her car outside the damn library at one o'clock in the morning working on a computer?

He stayed in his car, watching and waiting, for hours. She never got out, and nobody ever came to her. Just stared at the computer.

Finally, around 4:00 a.m., she turned her car back on and drove off. Tanner followed from behind, lights still off in his own vehicle, thankful he knew the roads well enough to drive this way.

But all she did was go back to her apartment.

Tanner stayed in his vehicle, lights still off, as she went inside. He was tempted to confront her right at this second, but he knew she wouldn't tell him anything.

She hadn't broken any laws, so he had no grounds

to officially question her anyway. The best he would have was loitering.

He wanted to pull on his hair. Why, on the one night in particular when she was supposed to get as much sleep as possible, would she spend half the night sitting in her car outside the library working on a computer?

Not meeting anyone. Not talking on that phone of hers.

There were too many things about her that didn't make sense.

Was this what his father had felt before the teenager he'd been trying to help fifteen years ago had ultimately turned on him and killed him? Dad had gone to pick up the kid in Denver, trying to get him out of a dire situation. Tanner's parents had sat Tanner and his siblings down the day before and told them the kid might be staying with them for a while. That sometimes helping a stranger was the right thing to do.

Then the kid had shot his dad, point-blank, when Dad showed up to help him. Trying to gain a foothold into the local gang.

The kid himself had been killed two days later in a shootout with the police when they'd come to arrest him.

Had Dad had any inclination that the kid was going to turn on him? Had he felt the storm brewing but decided to ignore it? Up until the second a Glock 17 was pressed against his forehead, had Dad thought everything was going to work out?

Tanner wasn't going to need a Glock against his own skin before he recognized the danger in front of him. He already saw it.

Bree Daniels might be spotless on paper, but she was damn well trouble in flesh and blood. Deadly, wrapped in big green eyes and a fragile appearance.

One Dempsey man had died because he'd refused to see the truth.

Tanner wouldn't be the second.

Chapter Seven

Bree knew Cheryl and Dan were disappointed in her the next morning when she arrived for work, eyes gritty with exhaustion like they'd been every day before.

She'd hoped to be able to get so much more accomplished last night while the twins had been with Cheryl and Dan. But she'd just been so tired.

She should've known better. The Organization discovered many years ago that sleep deprivation didn't work on her. It affected her mental facilities too much for her to be able to do delicate hacking work.

Ten years later it was still the same, even if she was the one depriving herself.

"Oh, honey," Cheryl crooned. Bree stood stiffly as the older woman hugged her. "What happened? You still look so tired. Maybe you should take the day off."

Dan patted her back, not nearly as outwardly affectionate as his wife, although Bree knew he also cared. "Could you still not sleep?" he asked.

Bree pulled back from Cheryl, unable to bear her touch. Not with the way she was feeling right now. "I guess it was just hard for me, being without the kids. I was worried."

That was true, but it wasn't the whole truth. She'd been glad Christian and Beth were with the Andrewses so she didn't have to drag them out in the middle of the night. But she'd desperately wanted to make more forward progress than she had.

The Wi-Fi at her apartment wasn't safe to use because her activities would lead the Organization directly to her. So she'd chosen the library, since the internet was hooked up through a government-issued router that she'd been able to hack in under two minutes, and the signal reached out to the parking lot. Using their system would keep her digital fingerprint from being traced back to any single computer—it would all just get hidden within the state of Colorado's virtual information flow.

But she hadn't been able to make any forward progress. She was too tired, or maybe she'd just lost her edge after being out of the hacking game for so long. Every day her skin itched and her mind burned with the knowledge of her failure.

It was just like being back inside the Organization all those years ago. When nothing she'd done had been good enough. When failure had meant pain and that people she'd cared about would suffer.

Was Melissa suffering?

Compounding all Bree's desperation was the knowledge that she was running out of time here. She felt eyes on her all the time.

Sometimes it was Tanner. She'd gotten used to his deep brown eyes watching her every time he was in here. Trying to figure out exactly what sort of threat she was to the people he was responsible for.

If he knew what sort of hell she could rain down on Risk Peak, he would've already escorted her to the county line.

But he didn't, so he watched and bided his time, piecing together what he could from what he observed. Determined to figure out her secrets.

She sensed other eyes on her, too. She could feel them day by day. And they didn't bring her a sense of comfort like Tanner's eyes did. They made her feel like she was being smothered.

But that didn't make sense. Why would anyone else be watching her? If it was the Organization, they would've made their move already. Killed her in her sleep if she was lucky. Dragged her back into hell if she wasn't.

So it wasn't the Organization. Bree drew in a shaky breath. That only left one option.

That she was following the same path of paranoia her mother had taken. That her mind was beginning to crumble in on itself the way Mom's had. She rubbed her shoulder again, at the wound her mother had given her the day her mind had snapped.

Maybe Bree's mind was snapping in the same way. Maybe somewhere down the road she was going to hurt the Andrewses or, worse, the twins, because her mind was convinced they were a threat.

She blinked rapidly and realized the older couple were both studying her now with abject concern. "I'm sorry, what?"

Cheryl gave Dan a worried look. "We're just wondering if you should take the day off, too. I'm sure we can manage."

She took a deep breath. "No, I'm fine." She was going to need the money if she had to leave suddenly. "I hope Christian and Beth were okay for you."

Cheryl smiled. "They were angels, as I knew they would be. Got up once during the night, but heck, Dan gets up more than that."

Bree was surprised how much she'd missed the kids, even though it had only been ten hours since she'd seen them last. Beth smiled sweetly like she always did, and even Christian was content in his carrier. Bree began rolling silverware in napkins while sitting at the corner "baby booth," but was soon scooted out of the way when some of Cheryl and Dan's friends came in and wanted to hold the babies.

The people in this town were so good. Bree didn't want to bring the Organization down on them. She had to be careful with her hacking. She was up against some of the most brilliant people on the planet, whose consciences were nonfunctional. They wouldn't hesitate to slaughter the people here if it would stop Bree.

She wasn't surprised when Tanner showed up a few minutes after she started her shift, looking just as haggard as she did. He didn't try to talk to her, like he usually did, just ordered breakfast and sat at his normal bar perch.

When she did catch sight of his brown eyes, they were hard. Cold, almost. No sign of the subtle invitation to reach out to him that she'd seen for the past week.

Or was that just her paranoia talking?

He ate his breakfast but then surprised her by not leaving afterward. He stayed put, pulling out a computer and starting to do some sort of work.

Bree ignored him, as always—a little easier today because of the frigid air that seemed to surround him. She did her duties in the back kitchen and helped out at lunch when a group of half a dozen construction workers came in.

Her paranoia ramped up once again with their arrival. She felt eyes on her all the time. But the only one she ever saw looking in her direction was Tanner.

She forced herself to shake off the feeling through the lunch rush and was clearing off the tables once the diner had nearly emptied when a buzzing noise caught her attention. She looked around, trying to figure out where it was coming from.

Then she realized it was coming from the phone in her apron.

She slammed the tray full of dishes down on the nearest table, wincing at the noise, thankful when nobody else seemed to notice. She started to hide the fact that she was looking at a message on her phone but realized that was absurd. People used phones all the time. No one would think twice about her getting a text. She flipped it open.

Come to Denver. Downtown Orthodox Church. 3:00. Crisscross, applesauce.

Bree stared at the message before snapping the phone closed. She couldn't even be sure it was from Melissa. Someone could've gotten hold of the phone and was trying to draw Bree out. Or maybe someone in the Organization was forcing Melissa to send the message.

No, Mellie wouldn't do that. She would die rather than risk the twins.

Right?

Bree stared at the phone again. She had to try. If this was Melissa's chance to get out, Bree couldn't let her down.

She couldn't take the twins with her into an unknown situation; if she had to run, it would be too hard with them in tow. Hopefully Dan and Cheryl would watch them again. She'd say she wasn't feeling well and needed to rest. She hated that they would so readily believe her just because they were honest people.

But Bree had to. She wouldn't let her paranoia suffocate her. And she at least knew the older couple would do whatever it took to keep Christian and Beth safe if Bree didn't come back.

She put the phone back in her apron and turned toward the kitchen, stopping in her tracks when she found Tanner studying her with hooded eyes.

"Everything okay?" he asked.

A bolt of panic jolted down her spine. Had he seen her get the message on her phone?

She forced air into her lungs and tried to relax her features. There was nothing suspicious about getting a text message. The only thing that would make it seem suspicious was her actions.

"Yes." She forced more air into her lungs so her voice didn't sound so weak. "Everything's fine."

"Get some news on your phone?" Tanner leaned back casually against the bar as he said it, but there was nothing casual about the way he studied her, reading every move she made.

She shrugged. "No. Just a junk sales message."

"Yeah, I hate those." He crossed his arms over his chest. "You look a little tired. I thought Mr. and Mrs. A were watching the babies for you last night so you could get some rest."

She fought the urge to shift back and forth on her feet. "I guess I just couldn't sleep anyway. You know how it is."

He cocked his head to the side. "I don't, actually. Why don't you tell me how it is? Did you go out?"

"Oh, no. I'm not big on nightlife stuff." She wasn't even sure if Risk Peak had any. "I just stayed home."

"But couldn't sleep, huh?"

Why was he so interested in her sleep habits? She didn't have time to talk to him about this. She needed to get to Denver, scope out as much as she could to make sure it was really Melissa who had contacted her.

"Yeah, just couldn't sleep. That's all. Do you need anything else, Officer?"

"Tanner." He reached over and touched her arm, just below her elbow. "Do *you* need anything, Bree? Tell me what's going on. I can help."

She looked into his eyes and almost believed him. Was tempted, maybe, because of the exhaustion, to tell him at least *something*. Not everything, of course, but enough to get his help.

He looked so strong. So capable. Like he could handle anything. While she woke every day not sure how she was going to make it, each day worse than the one before.

He waited silently, not pushing, not demanding. Which just made her want to lean on him more.

But she couldn't. Melissa might be getting out today, and they would have to run. She couldn't depend on anyone but herself.

"I'm fine," she finally said. "But thank you for asking."

Tanner didn't say anything, but his finger stroked lightly across the bend of her elbow. Once again her resolve almost faltered.

"Who was that message from, Bree?"

She didn't look him in the eye while shaking her head. "It was nobody."

She moved from his soft grip and walked back to the kitchen. She had to get the sexy deputy out of her mind. She needed to ask Dan and Cheryl to watch the kids, then get to Denver and meet her cousin.

And pray it wasn't a trap.

Chapter Eight

An hour and a half later, dressed in as much of a disguise as she could manage, which basically consisted of stuffing her long brown hair in a ball cap and sunglasses that covered a lot of her face, Bree sat in a bookstore across from the church where she was supposed to meet Melissa. She'd already been in the highest floors of the surrounding buildings that she could get to without raising suspicion, trying to do as much short-term recon as she could manage.

Everything about the city made her want to panic. Denver, for all the natural beauty of the surrounding mountains, was also a hub for technology. The public face of the Organization had an office here.

And the message from Melissa—the more Bree considered it, the worse it seemed. No doubt the phone was being tracked. Otherwise, how would Melissa know Bree could even make it to Denver in two hours?

If it was Melissa at all.

Hopefully, the Organization still thought she was dead and completely off their radar. Because the Organization's radar was a deadly place to be—particularly for her.

But Bree saw no sign of them now. Even after searching for over thirty minutes, Bree found no evidence of a trap. She stayed where she was at the bookstore until she finally spotted Melissa going into the church right on time for their meeting. Her cousin didn't look around, didn't draw attention to herself in any way. Just did the smart thing and went straight in.

Bree stood at the window, coffee cup in hand, waiting to see if there would be further movement. She watched for light reflecting from the roofs of the surrounding buildings, a sign of a sniper. She looked for any hint that someone was surveilling the scene rather than performing their task at hand: turning pages too slowly or too quickly, or staring at a display stand for too long.

But…nothing. Nothing suspicious or out of place.

Bree finally went around to the alley so she could enter through the side door of the church. Still keeping an eye out for any problems, she moved silently through it, finding Melissa sitting in an empty, darkened corner near two possible exits. It was exactly where Bree would've chosen if she had gotten here first.

Since she was already in a church, Bree sent up a prayer that this wasn't a trap and walked up to her cousin.

"Hi, Mellie."

Melissa spun toward her, pure joy on her face. But it quickly faded. "You didn't bring them."

The twins. Of course she would want to see them. "It wasn't safe. I wasn't sure of the situation. I can't move quickly enough with the two of them."

Melissa wiped quickly at her eyes. "I know. That was

smart, and the right thing to do. I'm just being emotional. But, God, Bree, I miss them so much."

Bree could definitely understand that. Those two little humans had a way of entrenching themselves into anybody's life. "They're getting so big. They're beautiful." Bree winced when Melissa's face fell even more—Bree was just making things worse. Meeting other people's emotional needs wasn't her forte. She tried to think of what might make her cousin feel better. "They're healthy, Mel. Happy."

"They're safe?"

Safe was definitely a relative term. She thought of the eyes she'd felt on her in Risk Peak. And the possibility that the Organization could be ready to move in on them even now.

Bree shrugged. "As safe as they can possibly be, given how you and I live. The older couple watching Beth and Christian love them. If something happened to me, they would take care of them to the best of their ability."

If Bree was better at personal stuff, she would probably pull her cousin in for a hug. But it would just be awkward for them both, so Bree quelled the urge.

Melissa wiped at tears again. "Thank you for taking them. I never planned to leave them alone with you—I thought I would be coming, too. I hope you've been all right."

She thought of all the sleepless nights. The running out of money. The sheer exhaustion and despair that had seemed like a constant companion for the past two months. Telling Melissa about how hard it had been wouldn't change anything. "We've managed."

"I just wish I could see pictures of them, you know? That you and I could be like any two other relatives in the world, where you pull out your phone and show me pictures of the kids."

They both knew that looking at pictures snapped on a smartphone would've been the worst possible thing they could do. It would lead the Organization right to them.

"Don't worry, I know it's impossible," Melissa continued. "I would never want you to put them in danger like that. To put yourself in danger like that."

"Is the Organization still capable of doing everything they were before?" It had been bad enough ten years ago when she'd escaped.

Melissa rubbed her forehead. "Worse and growing. They now have unfettered access to the pictures and sounds recorded on millions of phones. They've gotten smarter in the last ten years. Nobody suspects software that seems to make phones *better*."

Most people accepted that Big Brother might possibly be listening when they called or video chatted with someone. But they never considered that their phone's cameras and audio could still be transmitting even when they were in off mode.

That's what the Organization had spent all their energy developing. Ways of using people's phones when they weren't aware of it. Basically creating a worldwide information network that they controlled and no one knew about.

Melissa grabbed Bree's hand. "They finally figured out what they need to hack every phone on the planet. It's software that on the surface will look like it enhances video and audio quality of all phones. No one will be able to hide once it goes into operation on the phones."

This was worse than Bree thought. "But how are they gaining access to all the major phone manufacturers? They'll have to do it at once, or the companies will start to ferret out what they're doing."

Melissa shook her head, looking at Bree with wonder. "I should've known you would grasp the ramifications from the beginning. The Organization was so mad when they lost you, Bree. You set them back years by not having your genius around anymore. They knew that."

Bree just shook her head. If they'd had Bree around—controlled her and forced her to cooperate—the technological advances would've been astounding.

And all used for evil.

"The Organization doesn't need to get to all the cellular manufacturers. They are all coming here," Melissa continued. "To Denver."

"The International Tech Symposium."

"Yep. And guess who the sponsor is."

"Communication for All," Bree whispered.

The Organization was so much more insidious because of who the world thought they were—Communication for All, a charity focused on using technology to improve education and living conditions all over the world. And they did help millions of people.

But for a small core group of the charity, the endgame was far more nefarious than improving lives. They wanted to be able to control information. The charity front allowed them access and a lack of scrutiny that private companies would never be able to obtain.

Melissa shrugged. "Tech companies are so busy looking for malicious software, they just tend to overlook systems and software that makes their product better, especially when it comes from a world-renowned charity group. Plus, Communication for All is providing the new technology for free."

Bree muttered a curse. "And being hailed as heroes."

Melissa nodded. "All over the world. What's worse is that the new software also serves as a virus. Once it's uploaded to the manufacturers at the symposium, it will spread and download to every phone, regardless if people refuse to accept the update or not."

Bree sucked in a breath. "They finally figured out the way to use people's personal passwords to access their phones." It had been something they were trying to force her to help do years ago.

Melissa nodded. "Once they've done it, no one will be able to hide from their networks unless they pay to do so. They'll shelter whoever will pay their exorbitant fee and will be able to hunt whoever they desire."

Bree rubbed her eyes. "Now that sounds more like the Organization we know and hate."

They stared at each other for a few moments, both caught in a wave of despair.

"How did you keep them from finding out about the babies?" Bree finally asked.

"I was really sick early on in my pregnancy and didn't start gaining much weight until my fifth month."

"Then what did you do?"

"I followed your example. I got off the electronic grid completely. The Organization is convinced you're dead, Bree. For years they searched for you, even though you wiped all the pictures of you and your mom from the system before you ran. Only in the last couple of years did they give up."

"Why did they give up?"

Melissa shrugged. "I think they figured nobody living in this millennium could have resisted the lure of a smartphone or social media for that long. All they needed was one single picture on a smartphone, or even in the background of someone else's social media, and that would've been it. They would've known you were alive and they would've never stopped hunting you."

So her mother's paranoia had kept them alive after all.

"What you did was brilliant," Melissa continued.

Bree shrugged. "I'm not sure *brilliant* was the word for it." Lonely. Nerve-racking. So damn hard.

"Whatever it was, it worked for you, so I decided to try it." A sadness fell across Melissa's face. "The Organization killed the twins' father before I knew I was pregnant. I think they suspected I was going to make a move against them, and this was their way of letting me know they weren't afraid to play hardball." She swallowed rapidly.

"I'm so sorry, Mellie."

"Me, too. I never got to say goodbye to him. They ran his car off the road and tried to act like they had nothing to do with it. They sent me an obnoxiously large bouquet of flowers. That's how I knew they were behind it. But you know what? It was the best thing they could've done. Because it reminded me that I could play hardball, too."

There was a fire in her cousin's eyes.

"The loss of my fiancé, Christian, ended up giving me the excuse I needed to take a few months off and get away from them."

"Christian." Bree couldn't help but smile at the name.

Melissa's smile was tinged with sadness. "Yes, he went by Chris, but his full name was Christian. I named the twins after the two people I love most in the world."

Bree reached out and touched Melissa's arm. It felt stiff and unnatural, but Melissa didn't seem to mind.

"The Organization just let you go?"

"No, of course not. I kept working. But I did it from a remote location. They were tracking me to see if I would do something to hurt the company, not for anything as mundane as pregnancy. And that's going to be their downfall—the fact that they're so narrow and conceited in their focus."

"They don't understand the concept of family." Neither did Bree, if she was honest.

Melissa nodded. "I used their information system against them. I didn't have the babies in the hospital, and I made sure all social media and pictures from my phones created the narrative I wanted. One that gave no suggestion of their birth, just that I was grieving the death of my lover."

"You outstrategized them." Bree smiled and nodded. "Good for you."

Melissa smiled. "I was never what you were. Never a prodigy. They tried to make me into you, but I was never good enough. You think like a computer, Bethany. I never did. My emotions got in my way."

Bree knew her cousin meant the words as a compliment. But the knowledge that she was colder, harder, more machinelike tore at her, at a level she wasn't really aware had existed before the babies came into her life.

She had feelings, too. They weren't easy to process or express, but she had them.

"Once the Organization's new system takes hold, it will be nearly impossible for you to hide," Melissa said. "You've been so careful, but rumors are flying again that you're still alive. You're the ghost in their machine."

Bree sighed. "I've been trying to poke at their system through a back door with the files you gave me. They shouldn't have been able to tell it was me."

"I've been covering for you as much as possible. Anything that looked like it was coming from Colorado, I rerouted, but I think they're onto you, or me. I'm not sure which."

Bree looked around at a phantom sound. She didn't see anyone, but that didn't mean no one was there. "Do you think someone followed you here?"

Melissa nodded. "I'm sure they did, but I bought us enough time to meet. I've made it common practice to duck into churches—it's part of the narrative I've set up to help deceive the Organization. So they won't find it uncommon for a while."

Bree shook her head in wonder. Melissa might not have had the natural programming and coding skills Bree possessed, but the woman was brilliant in her own right, evident by the way she'd fooled the Organization these last few months.

"But that's why I wanted to meet," Melissa continued. "You haven't been able to make much progress with the files, have you?"

"Unfortunately, taking care of two infants and working full-time has been taking up a lot of my attention."

Melissa grabbed Bree's hand and squeezed it, tears in her eyes once again. "Thank you, for all you're doing. I wish it was me up all night with them. But you have to stop digging into the files. The Organization is too suspicious."

"I'm trying to be as secretive as I can. I don't think I've left any footprints that could be traced back to Risk Peak."

Melissa squeezed her hand again. "That's part of the problem. You're too good. They know someone is attempting access but aren't sure who or where. There aren't many people in the world who can breeze in and out undetected the way you can."

Bree was about to protest when Melissa's next words stopped her. "Michael Jeter came to see me last week."

Bree's entire body stiffened at the mention of the head of Communication for All. He had been the one who had recruited Bree when she was a child, and he had made her life a living hell when she'd refused to cooperate.

"He came to see you personally?" That was never good.

Melissa rolled her eyes. "The official reason he gave was to offer condolences about Chris's death, even though it was a year later. He wanted to make sure I was doing all right, since he knew I didn't have any family."

"But you didn't buy it?"

"Not even for a second. He was there to fish out whether I was in touch with you. And then, as a 'gift'—" Melissa put the word in air quotes "—they were giving me one of the first completely upgraded computer systems. They took mine without a word. If I'd had anything on there..."

She didn't finish, but she didn't have to. They hadn't given Melissa any warning or time to erase anything on her hard drive. If her computer had contained any trace of communication with Bree, they would've known about it.

Michael Jeter showing up himself just confirmed how suspicious they really were.

"There was nothing on there that could've led them to me and the kids?"

"Nothing. This is the only thing I use to communicate with your phone." She held out a phone that looked similar to Bree's—old with no camera. "I tracked you using a public system outside the Organization. But once this new system goes live, they'll find you, Bree. It will only be a matter of time."

"Okay, I'll work harder on the files you gave me." She didn't know how she would find the time and energy, but she would make it happen.

"No. That's the opposite of what needs to happen. I'll focus on the Organization files. You just keep off the grid and keep the kids safe."

"But—"

Melissa's phone buzzed in her hand.

"We're out of time," she said. "You need to get out right away. I'll go out the front and draw them away. You go out the side."

Bree grabbed Melissa's hand. "Are you going to be able to decode the files before the summit? Especially with them watching you?"

"I have to. That's all there is to it. Your job is to keep yourself and the babies safe. That's the most important thing. Nobody knows about Risk Peak, so just stay there and stay out of it."

Before Bree knew what was happening, Melissa pulled her in for a hug. Bree stiffened before forcing herself to relax into it. This was her cousin. They'd hugged each other as children. Melissa had been the only person who'd ever really befriended the stiff, difficult Bree.

"You're doing a great job with the kids," Melissa whispered in her ear. "Thank you."

They pulled away from each other as a door slammed in the back.

"Mellie, be careful."

"The twins are the only thing that matters. If something happens to me..."

Bree wasn't going to offer useless platitudes. She nodded. "The twins are the only thing that matters," she repeated. "I'll make sure they're safe, first and foremost."

They squeezed each other's hand, then Melissa's phone buzzed again and she rushed toward the front door.

Bree kept to the shadows, moving faster when she heard a man's voice talking on the phone in the hallway behind her, a priest saying something about communion for the next Mass. She crouched behind a pew and waited for the voice to move past, relieved when he didn't seem to slow at all near her. She made her way to the side door she'd come in through.

She slid the door open quietly and stepped back into

the alley. Glancing both ways, she turned and walked rapidly in the opposite direction from the way she'd come.

It looked like she was going to make it out of the city alive after all.

She was about to round the corner into the larger avenue when a hand reached out from the shadows, covered her mouth and yanked her hard against the wall.

Chapter Nine

Tanner kept his hand tightly over Bree's mouth and pushed her harder against the wall. Her back went ramrod straight, and he knew it would only be a split second before she panicked and started fighting him.

Which was definitely going to draw the attention of the three armed men less than twenty feet away. Bree had been about to walk into them.

"Bree." His voice was so low it was almost silent. It was only because his mouth was right against her ear that she'd be able to hear him. "It's Tanner."

Her body relaxed enough that he at least knew she understood him and didn't think of him as a threat.

He couldn't help but be aware of all the feminine curves pushed up against him, but he forced those thoughts from his mind.

He loosened his hand on her mouth just the slightest bit. "We've got trouble. Do you understand?"

She nodded.

He heard footsteps and pushed up against her more tightly, making sure he was between her and the guys he'd seen carrying weapons at their waists a few minutes ago.

She pulled at his hand. He let her mouth go, and she immediately began wiggling around, shifting her small body until they were front to front.

Perfect—if ignoring the sexy back curves of this beautiful woman wasn't hard enough, now he had to ignore sexy front curves also.

He brought his finger up to his lips, and she nodded once more. He tucked her more firmly up into the doorway corner, drawing his own weapon from its holster.

It wasn't the best odds against three armed men, but it was better than nothing.

"Where is she?" one voice said from about ten feet away now. If the men shifted much closer, they would practically fall over him and Bree.

"She didn't come down my way. We had both exits covered," another voice said. "Did you see her inside?"

Bree stiffened as the third man responded. "I just got in there, since we were given the wrong info. I had to take care of the priest so he didn't wander out and see anything."

"Dead?"

"No. Seemed unnecessary. Unconscious. Weathers was talking to someone, but I didn't get there in time to see who."

All three men got quiet as a phone rang.

"Hello, Mr. Jeter," guy number one said.

Bree began breathing rapidly and was all but trembling in Tanner's arms now. What the hell was going on?

"We followed Ms. Weathers to a church in Denver. It looks like she was talking to someone, but we're not sure who."

Tension continued to rocket through Bree's slender body as the person on the other end spoke.

"No, sir," the first man finally replied. "No positive ID or pictures. We're working on that now."

Another pause.

"No, I don't think coming here yourself is a good option."

The trembling in Bree's limbs became more pronounced.

"By the time you got here, the scene would be cold. Let us continue to search. It might have been a random stranger. Ms. Weathers has been known to stop and talk to people since the accident." He paused.

"Yes, sir. We'll keep looking and keep you posted." He obviously disconnected the call. "If we don't want the boss here trying to do our job for us and handing us our asses, let's find out who Weathers was talking to."

"Maybe she's still in the church. Whoever it was couldn't have gotten far," the third voice said.

The men's voices began to fade as they walked back toward the church door.

"The third one was inside the church," Bree whispered. "He was on the phone, talking about communion. He walked not five feet away from me."

"And if he had found you?" Tanner whispered in her ear.

She didn't say anything. Had he really expected her to? At least she wasn't shaking anymore.

He was going to have answers, but first they needed to get out of here.

A few moments later, he stepped back from her and took her hand, and they moved quickly together down the alley. As soon as they were at an open corner, relatively safe since people were around everywhere, he grabbed his phone.

"I've got to call this in."

He wasn't prepared for the utter panic that blanketed her features. She grabbed his wrist with both of her hands.

"No. Tanner, please."

He shook his head. "Those men were armed. You heard them. One said he hurt the priest. Were they going to hurt you if they had found you?"

She nodded slowly.

"Then I need to call this in," he continued. "I don't know why you're protecting them, but it ends now."

"I'm not protecting them. I'm protecting *me*. If you call this in, I'm as good as dead."

"Because you're on the run."

Her face was ashen, huge green eyes dwarfing the rest of her features. "Yes, but not from the law."

It was the first time she'd admitted there was something bad going on with her.

He shook his head. "I can't do nothing."

She rubbed her fingers over her eyes. "I know this is going to sound crazy, but can you drive to the nearest police station and tell them in person rather than call?"

He shook his head. "That will take too long. The priest might need medical attention. What if I call anonymously? I can even call the police department directly, so they won't trace the call like they do 911 calls. I won't give them my name."

He would do it, even though it went against his code as a law enforcement officer.

"No, they'll still be able to link it back to your phone. And it will draw even more attention because you didn't do what was expected." She began to look around frantically. "Plus, being here in Denver at the exact same time. They'd be stupid not to put that together."

"Exact same time as what? And who is *they*?"

"You're only going to believe me if I show you."

Tanner wanted to throw up his hands in frustration. "Bree." He put his hands on both her arms. "Show me *what*?"

"Do you trust me?"

He rolled his eyes. "About as far as I can throw you."

"Well, do you think you could throw me across that street?" She pointed at a man who was talking on his phone, standing at a coffee shop kitty-corner from the church.

"What do you want me to do?"

"Go to that man. Get him to call 911 and tell them the priest is in trouble. But as soon as he does it, you've got to get out of sight. They're in the area, so it won't take them long to pinpoint the location of the call. So have the guy make the call, then get back over here quickly."

This was a lot of cloak-and-dagger stuff even for a cop. But he had no doubt Bree's fear was real.

"You stay right here." He pointed to the ground. He wanted her where he could see her.

She shook her head. "I can't be out here. I can't be around anybody else when this happens. They'll immediately utilize every cell phone in a half-mile grid."

Tanner gritted his teeth. Before this day was over, he was going to understand what the hell she was talking about. "Remember that part about not as far as I can throw you?"

"If you don't trust me, can you at least trust that I want to get back to the twins without leading any sort of danger to them?"

He grimaced, but he had to agree. Bree wouldn't do anything to hurt the babies. They were wasting time. He nodded at her, and she took off to a little park with no people around.

Tanner jogged over to the man still glancing at his phone in front of the church. He pulled out his badge. This would be the easiest way.

"Excuse me." He flashed his badge in front of the guy. "My phone just broke and I need you to call 911. We've got a priest inside who passed out and injured himself."

The guy's eyes got big. "Are you serious, man? Sure, no problem."

Tanner stayed long enough to make sure the guy was really calling, then slipped away toward the park.

And didn't see Bree there.

Damn it, had she run? He was on his way to getting well and truly angry when she stuck her head out from behind a large tree and gestured frantically for him to come over. He just made it to her, and was about to read her the riot act, when a car—*multiple* cars—came screeching up behind him, pulling right up on the guy who had called 911.

"What the hell?" Bree's slender arm grabbed his shirt and yanked him behind the tree with her.

There was no way emergency response could've gotten there that fast, less than a minute after the call. And even if they had, they wouldn't have wasted their time going to the guy on the phone when there was a possibly injured man inside the church.

Tanner peeked out to see the men in suits questioning the 911 caller. Bree was between him and the tree, her back to him, but she wasn't looking. She already knew who was there.

"Those are the same guys from the alley, right?"

She nodded.

"How did they get there so fast?" Tanner asked. "Are they tracing 911 calls or something?"

"No, it wouldn't have mattered what number he called. He was flagged because he mentioned the priest in the church. Only a witness would've known about the priest."

Tanner looked again before pulling his head back. "Those men are dangerous. Are they going to hurt that guy?" He couldn't sit by and let an innocent bystander get hurt.

She shook her head. "Not when they find out someone else asked him to make the call. It won't take them long to figure out he's not who they want. You are."

"Fine. They can have me. I'm law enforcement. I can call in Denver PD backup and we can arrest them. We'll end this right now."

She let out a small laugh that held no humor whatsoever. "Those guys are nothing more than hired guns. Arresting them wouldn't accomplish anything."

"It would be a start. I've got at least one admitting to hurting the priest."

"If you arrest them, you'll be bringing danger right to my doorstep. To Christian and Beth's doorstep."

He snatched his head back behind the tree as the 911 caller pointed in their general direction. The men in the suits evidently wanted to know who had asked him to make the call.

"We've got trouble," he said. "We're going to have to run."

She nodded. "I can keep up."

She wasn't lying. They moved from tree to tree, using the natural park coverage for as long as they could. And then they bolted. He heard a shout from behind them, and they pushed faster.

Tanner was in good shape, kept himself physically fit for the job and because it was how he liked to feel. Even with Bree's assurances, he thought he would have to slow down significantly for her to be able to keep up with him.

He was wrong.

Bree was with him almost step for step. Was actually running faster because her shorter gait meant more steps. She was definitely very much in shape.

They circled back around on the outside of the park, cutting sharply to the left down a crowded avenue.

"If anyone has their phone out, try to keep your face averted," she panted. "It's important that they don't catch your picture."

"If we don't want anyone getting us on picture or video, we're much better off blending in rather than bolting through."

She stopped running almost immediately. "You're right. Damn it, you're right."

It was like she was mad at herself for breaking a rule she knew about.

They kept moving quickly, but not fast enough to be interesting to any passersby. Tanner glanced over his shoulder and saw two of the men in suits turning down the avenue. They obviously weren't sure exactly who they were looking for, and their progress was slower because they had to look more closely at everyone.

"We should split up," Bree said.

"No way in hell." He reached down and wrapped her hand in his, a little afraid she might bolt.

"They're looking for a couple. Separating is logical. We could meet up later when it's safe."

"But it also makes us more vulnerable." He wasn't worried about himself, he was worried about her. "What would happen if they caught you?" He held her hand more tightly in his, ignoring the relief he felt when she didn't try to pull away.

"I'd probably be dead before my body hit the ground," she murmured.

Damn it. "Then we definitely stay together."

They ducked around a family, and Bree turned more fully to him, putting her hand on his forearm and squeezing. "It's me they want, not you. You don't have to be in danger. This isn't your fight."

He shook his head. "We stay together."

She looked like she wanted to argue further, but there was no time.

When Tanner saw a suit enter the crowded street from the other direction, conspicuous because of his obvious observation of everyone, he wrapped an arm around Bree and pulled her into the nearest shop.

"Someone just entered the street from the other end. Waiting them out is probably our best bet."

She nodded. "We need to find somewhere away from people. They'll start scanning phones soon."

He didn't know exactly what that meant, but it didn't sound good. "Mine, too?"

"No, your flip phone is too old. It's safe."

Thank God Grand County was behind the times when it came to updating communication devices.

Bree looked around the general discount store they'd entered and began pulling him toward the back and the restrooms, then into the separate handicapped bathroom that would give them full privacy. Tanner grabbed an out-of-order sign resting under the water fountain and hung it on the door's hook as they went inside before shutting and locking the door behind him.

Bree closed the toilet seat lid and sat down wearily. "This is one of the best places we could've probably picked to hide. But we'll have to stay here probably an hour to make sure they've given up. Hopefully by then they'll just assume they lost us."

Tanner leaned back against the sink. "Good. That should give us enough time for you to tell me exactly what's going on. Starting with who those babies belong to. Because you're sure as hell not their biological mother."

Chapter Ten

Bree stared at Tanner as he leaned up against the sink, his long legs stretched out in front of him and strong arms crossed over his chest.

How much could she tell him? Definitely not the whole truth. First of all, he was law enforcement. Under oath to fight bad guys or whatever. Knowing Tanner and his sense of justice, he would want to take on the Organization all by himself. The only thing that would succeed in doing was getting him killed.

If he even believed her at all. Why would anybody believe that a charity organization that had helped millions of underprivileged and impoverished people gain access to education and technology was actually housing a terrorist group buying and selling privacy and information?

Communication for All was the perfect front. They seemed so pure and altruistic in their motives.

No, she definitely couldn't tell him everything she knew. But she had to tell him something.

"Christian and Beth aren't my children. You're right. They belong to my cousin, Melissa."

"Melissa Weathers. The woman you met today at

the church, and who the suits were talking about on the phone."

"How did you know I met her? How are you here at all?"

"I've been watching you carry around that phone every day since you got to town like it held the secrets to the known universe, but you never actually talk or text anyone on it. Then today you get a text and ten minutes later you're bolting out the door. So I followed you."

He was a cop. A damn good one, she knew that. She shouldn't be surprised. "Ok, fine. The text was from Melissa, telling me to meet her."

"But you still scoped out the place. I watched you do that, too. Quite proficiently, I might add. Do you not trust her?"

This was where it got tricky. How to give Tanner enough info that he would be satisfied, but not so much that he felt like he needed to step in and save the world. "No, I trust her. But she's gotten in with some bad people. She didn't want the twins around them, so she asked me if I could take care of them for a while."

"And those are the same people we're hiding from now? The ones in the alley, who also hurt the priest? I thought those were just the hired muscle. They work for the Mr. Jeter on the phone. Is that the person who was able to get the cars to the 911 call so quickly?"

He was studying her too closely and had way too many details. She had to derail him. "Yes, the group Melissa is trying to get away from is really good with technology and has found a way to triangulate cell phone signals to locate people. Something to do with multilateration and hybrid positioning systems."

Most people's eyes started to glaze over any time technical terms came into play. But Tanner's didn't. He might not have understood what she was saying, but she had no doubt he would be further researching it.

Fine. Everything she was telling him was vague enough that he wouldn't draw attention from the Organization if he started searching the terms. And when the terms didn't really lead him anywhere useful, he wouldn't blame her. After all, why would she know specifics about triangulation?

It wasn't like she had helped design the technology when she was thirteen years old or anything.

"And that's it? It's some sort of technologically savvy group of general bad guys she's in trouble with?"

Yeah, it sounded ridiculous when he said it like that. But Bree nodded. "Pretty much."

"So you agreed to watch the twins to help her out?"

"Yes, she was afraid if they knew where the twins were, they would take them and force her to do more work for them."

At least that much was true.

Tanner's eyes narrowed. "If this group is so technologically advanced and wants your cousin, wouldn't they know to come after you first?"

Damn it, this man was too intelligent for his own good.

"We had a falling-out years ago and hadn't talked to each other in a decade. That's why she came to me, because there were no ties to be found."

Mostly because the Organization thought she was dead.

He was studying her with those brown eyes that

never seemed to miss anything. She couldn't tell how much he was believing and how much he wasn't. There wasn't much more she could tell him.

She just needed him to let her lie low while Melissa tried to figure it out.

She ignored the voice in her head that told her that was never going to happen. That there was no way Melissa was a match for the Organization and would be able to crack the files she'd stolen, not when they were already a little suspicious of her.

Bree's heart hurt for her cousin. Hurt for the fact that she lost Christian—another victim of the Organization, just like her mother. Hurt that Melissa was missing seeing her babies get bigger day by day. Hurt that if Melissa didn't stop the Organization in time, all of this would be for naught anyway.

"What? What is it you're thinking right now?" She blinked rapidly as Tanner's thumb trailed gently down her cheek. She hadn't even realized he'd moved, but he was crouching beside her.

She couldn't tell him any of this. She wanted to—so desperately she wanted to share this burden, but she couldn't. Risk Peak needed him. He was a good man, and she refused to sign his death warrant.

But she couldn't seem to quite make herself pull away from his touch, either.

"I just want everything to be okay, but I don't see any way that that's going to happen."

"I can help. I might not be able to do anything as law enforcement in Risk Peak, but I've got contacts. Federal law enforcement. Colorado Springs is the headquarters for Omega Sector, a specialized task force equipped to handle this sort of thing. I know people there. I can help you and your cousin."

He said it with such conviction that she couldn't help but believe him. For just a moment, she almost caved. But she had no proof. Nobody would believe the word of a woman who was a ghost over that of a charity that had helped thousands and thousands of people.

"I have to give Melissa time. She's the only one who knows all the details of what's going on." She looked away as she told the lie, but his thumb was still gentle against her cheek.

"There's more, Bree. I know there's more you're not telling me."

She'd never had anyone be this gentle with her before. Not just the touch, but the patience. The concern.

Her mom, before the paranoia had completely taken her mind, had loved Bree—loved her enough to risk her own life. But she'd always been gruff, worried, scared.

Tanner Dempsey was none of those things.

His fingers seemed to burn against her skin. She had to pull away.

But there was more truth she could give him.

"I'm afraid I'm ruining those kids. I'm not good with people, anyone can see that." It was one of the things she liked about computers. With technology there was no emotional subtext. Coding was straightforward, logical, decisive. She didn't have to worry about nuances and emotional harm. "If Melissa had any other choice, she wouldn't have chosen me to care for Christian and Beth, believe me."

He shook his head. "Anyone can tell that you love

those children, Bree. They are not missing out on anything, especially not affection."

"Then how come Christian cries all the time?"

She meant it as a distraction, but as the words came out, she realized it was a true fear. Why would Christian cry all the time if he was getting what he needed?

"Some babies just cry more than others."

"Maybe he's smart enough to subconsciously realize I'm not as good as his mother and that his developmental needs aren't being met because his caretaker is emotionally stunted."

Tanner chuckled before his hands cupped her face and his lips touched hers briefly, lightly, before pulling away. "Or maybe the kid is just colicky."

He stood, backing away. Bree's fingers touched her lips where his had just been. He'd meant it as a kiss of camaraderie, encouragement. A show of support.

What would he think if he knew that was the first time she'd ever been kissed by a man in her entire life?

Then maybe he'd be more likely to agree with her about the emotional stuntedness.

"I want to help your cousin, Bree," he said. "And you. Because as long as they're willing to hurt other people to force her to do what they want, you're not safe. I can't turn a blind eye to that."

She couldn't let him start digging into it. "Just give her more time. She's gathering the evidence she needs, and when she has it, she'll go to the police."

Or they would run. Either way, it wouldn't be his problem anymore.

His dark brows furrowed together. "Doing nothing, knowing there's danger out there, doesn't sit well with me."

Now she stood and grabbed his hand. "I just need somewhere to lie low and keep the babies safe. Risk Peak is a good place to do that. No one is looking for me there."

She thought about her paranoia and the eyes she always felt on her there. But that couldn't be the Organization, so she would just have to keep it under control.

"Fine." Tanner nodded. "I'll let it go for now. But you can bet that I'm going to be sticking to you like glue, Bree Daniels. If someone is coming for you or those babies, they'll have to go through me first."

She didn't know if the fluttering in her chest was relief or panic.

Chapter Eleven

Over the next two weeks, Bree learned what normal life was supposed to be like.

She felt like she was back in the sitcom again, except this time she had a little more understanding of her role. She worked, played with the babies and got a good night's sleep each night.

But she had to keep reminding herself that this was just pretend. None of it—not the job, not the kids, not the man who came and walked her home from work every night—was real.

Eventually the season would be over and she would go back to what she had been before.

Alone.

"You've got an order up, Bree," Dan called out from the kitchen. Bree had moved up from jack-of-all-trades to regular lunch shift waitress. It was better for everyone. The Andrewses didn't have to pay her so much under the table, and she was able to make more money overall. Although now that she wasn't preparing to leave town as soon as possible, money wasn't so much of an issue.

But she wondered daily how it was going for Melissa. The phone had remained steadily silent in the two weeks since she'd last seen her cousin. Bree still had no way of getting in touch with her and no idea how the plan was going.

Not being an active part of the plan was difficult. Bree had always been someone who had plans, backup plans and backups to her backup plans. Ironically, it had been Michael Jeter who had first recognized that her mind worked like a flowchart. He'd been the one to help her develop that part of her brain, so that she was now able to see multiple scenarios at any given time.

She could see multiple scenarios for this situation also, but few of them ended well for Melissa, the twins or herself.

"Thanks, Dan." She grabbed the plate and took it out to the diners, glancing over where Judy sat with the babies.

They'd worked out a sort of schedule where someone could be keeping an eye on the twins whenever they were awake. Sometimes it was the other waitress, Judy, sometimes Dan or Cheryl, depending on the needs of the diner at the time.

Tanner had sat beside her as she'd told Dan and Cheryl that the babies weren't actually hers. Surprisingly, they hadn't seemed to care at all. The kids hadn't been kidnapped, and they still needed to be held and cared for. That was all that mattered to the older couple.

Bree forced a smile onto her face as she delivered the plates up for order. It was the construction crew again. More specifically, the skinny man with dark hair and dark eyes. She'd finally pinpointed him as the one who'd been watching her.

He never talked to her, never tried to get her to engage in conversation like some of the other workers did. Just watched her silently.

Everything about him made her want to take the babies and run. But she was determined not to let the paranoia take over her mind. This man could not be in the Organization. He would've already made his move.

She almost believed that, except for when all the doubts crept in.

Maybe the Organization was just biding its time.

Maybe they were waiting for Melissa to contact her so they could catch them both.

Maybe they had something so nefarious planned that Bree couldn't possibly imagine it.

She closed her eyes and shook the thoughts away. Maybe the guy was just awkward and rude and his parents had never taught him it was impolite to stare.

She had to let it go. She had real battles to fight. She didn't need to make up pretend ones in her head.

But as she delivered his food, she could swear the guy was planning to lock her in his basement to be his forever bride. She nodded at him and his buddies and backed away.

She took another order then walked back to the kitchen.

"Your creepy guy give you any problems?" Cheryl asked.

Bree shrugged. "Studied me with his creepy eyes and gave his creepy nod when I handed him his food."

"So basically acted the way he always does." Dan flipped a burger as he talked.

"Listen, buddy." Bree pointed at him after hanging

her order on the spinning wheel. "Don't be bringing logic where it doesn't belong. Leave me and my paranoia alone."

Dan chuckled, and Cheryl rubbed Bree's shoulder. Two weeks ago Bree would've shifted away from the touch. But she was learning. Learning that touching could be normal. That it was okay to joke with people.

"I think he's just a strange guy," Cheryl said.

"That's for sure," Bree muttered. But they were right. Just because he was strange didn't mean he was dangerous.

If she wanted to be able to live any sort of normal life, she was going to have to accept that. Not every strange stranger was dangerous. Not every stranger was from the Organization.

Bree grabbed the pitcher of water and walked back into the dining room to refill empty glasses. The front doorbell rang as someone came in, and a few moments later Bree felt eyes on her again.

But these she knew. And they belonged to someone who was very definitely not a creepy, thin man.

A smile rose to her lips unbidden.

She should not be smiling when it came to Tanner. Should not be thinking about him as much as she was. Should definitely not be dreaming about him at night, wondering what a real kiss from him might feel like.

She was doing her best to keep her distance, but Tanner made it so damn difficult. He just had something about him that drew people in. People trusted him, knew he would look out for them. The entire town of Risk Peak depended on him.

Bree had met his mother, sister and something ridiculous like eighty-seven cousins. Tanner had more family in a quarter-block radius from the diner than Bree had known her whole life.

He was smart, focused and determined to help her out of this mess.

He was everything she should run from. He already knew too much about her and the situation.

Yet she counted the minutes every day until he would be back and she could see him again.

He was here for at least one meal every day. Today it was lunch. At first she'd tried letting Judy or one of the other waitresses take his table, but he'd shut that down immediately. Now everyone knew he only wanted her.

His words, not hers.

And they did funny things to her insides.

He had another police officer with him today—not Ronnie Kitchens, the deputy who sometimes came in with Tanner. This guy was younger, a little chubby, wearing his brown sheriff's uniform like he wasn't quite comfortable with the fit.

Probably because the guy looked like he couldn't be but half a day out of police officer school, or whatever it was called.

Bree grabbed a couple of glasses of water and brought them out to Tanner's table.

"Hi." She set the glasses down and looked everywhere but at Tanner's face. She knew darn well what he looked like. Those brown eyes had been starring front and center in her dreams for the last two weeks.

"Hey. How's your day going? Twins sleep all right last night?"

She felt his fingers against her hand where it was

still wrapped around his glass of water. "Yeah. Even Christian slept five hours in one stretch."

She slipped her hand away from his and stuck both of them in the back pockets of her jeans, still staring down at the glasses.

Her withdrawal didn't seem to faze Tanner at all. "Five hours. That's a record for that little guy, isn't it?"

Now she looked him in the face, drawn in immediately by those deep brown eyes like she'd known she would be.

The moment stretched out between them.

"Hey there," he whispered, smiling, just like he had every day when she finally broke down and met his eyes. He was always patient, never frustrated that she found it hard to interact with him.

"You have twins? Holy cow!" Baby-face cop's booming question broke the moment. She looked away from Tanner and over at him. "I couldn't imagine having one baby, much less two. I'm Scott Watson. Nice to meet you."

She shook his outstretched hand as he grinned at her. "I'm Bree."

"Scott is on an intercounty task force. He's been traveling around to different departments, helping to regulate social media, reports, general communication with the public. He'll be here a week or so."

"I volunteered." Scott grinned. "Gives me a chance to meet people from all over Colorado. See towns and counties I might not get regular interaction with otherwise."

"No offense," Bree said, "but you almost don't seem old enough to be traveling around by yourself."

Scott chuckled, and the sound was so contagious Bree had to smile, too. "I know! I get that all the time. I wanted to do undercover work, but I was told they didn't get much call for chubby middle school kids undercover." He patted his smooth, round cheeks.

"I'll admit, I was a little irritated when I got the email about your arrival yesterday," Tanner said.

"Yesterday?" Scott's smile turned into a scowl. "You should've received the memo from the task force at least a month ago."

"Ends up I did, almost five weeks ago. Somehow it ended up in my junk mail."

"I'm still sorry. This sort of miscommunication is one of the things I'm trying to help eliminate. And I promise I won't be in your way. Just stuff me in an office under the stairs. Of course, if you have any action going on, I'd love to be a part of that, too."

Tanner just smiled. "We'll see."

Bree took their orders—Scott's choice of the pancake stack was not going to help his chubby middle school kid persona—when Tanner grabbed her hand again.

"I see who's back." He gestured toward the creepy, thin guy's table with his head. "You have any problems with him?"

She shook her head. "No. Nothing concrete, as usual."

Tanner stood. "I'm just gonna go chat with them."

Bree grabbed Tanner's hand. "He didn't say or do anything. Really."

His thumb trailed across her wrist. "I'm not going to

make a big deal. It never hurts for a deputy to say hello to people who work in town."

Tanner walked over to their table while Bree headed to the server station to get some coffee. When she brought the two mugs back, Tanner was still over talking to the construction guys.

"This is some really pretty country," Scott said. "Some of my favorite so far. Are you like Tanner—lived here all your life?"

Bree wasn't sure how much of her story he'd told Scott. Probably not much, if anything. They'd agreed to stick with a cover story of a violent ex-boyfriend if anyone ever really needed information.

"No, I've just moved here recently. Needed to get out of the situation I was in."

She looked over at Tanner. What was he saying to the men? She didn't trust the creepy guy, but neither was she trying to disrupt the whole town.

A few seconds later, Tanner turned and walked back to his table.

"Don't worry, I didn't say anything about you. Just chatting with them about the building progress. Normal Risk Peak stuff."

"Okay." She let out a sigh. "I'm probably being paranoid."

"I know I don't know what's going on," Scott said. "But sometimes it's good to be a little paranoid in this world. Even chubby middle schoolers know that."

Scott's rueful smile had her feeling better. She walked back to the kitchen to place their order.

But when she looked over her shoulder, creepy guy was staring at her again.

"ARE THE CONSTRUCTION workers giving your lady friend a hard time?"

Tanner watched as Bree walked back into the kitchen then glanced over to find that the man in question was indeed watching her.

He'd told her the truth about the talk he'd had with the guys—it had been friendly, neutral. No threats, veiled or otherwise.

But it had been a reminder that Tanner was here. Was always around. That anything that happened in this town was going to go through him. And he especially wasn't going to let anything happen to Bree.

He didn't think the creepy, thin guy had any dubious intent toward her, but he made Bree uncomfortable, which was enough for Tanner to make his presence known. Since there weren't any laws he was breaking just by looking at her, there wasn't much more Tanner could do other than that.

Sticking close to her hadn't been a problem. True to his word in that bathroom two weeks ago, Tanner had made sure he was around.

He knew she hadn't told him the full truth that day. There were still huge chunks of info about her situation he didn't have. But trying to force or bully the truth out of her would just cause her to shut down and withdraw. She would revert into that thick shell of hers.

So for the past two weeks he'd been trying to *gentle* the truth out of her.

This prickly woman had plenty of defenses against someone trying to force her to do something, but she seemed clueless when it came to someone being kind to her.

Of course, he should probably put her in protective custody. That would be the safest thing for both her and the babies. And he still might have to do that.

He grimaced at the thought. Bree would hate it. Would hate him.

But at least she would be safe.

"Tanner?"

Tanner brought his attention back to Scott. The younger man looked concerned. Having anybody shadowing the department was an annoyance, but at least Scott was easygoing and likable so far.

Tanner shook his head. "The construction guys aren't going to be a problem. Bree is just a little skittish."

Scott took a sip of his coffee. "She said she just moved here a few weeks ago. She running from something?"

Tanner sipped his own. "What makes you say that?"

"I may have only been on the force for eight months, but my deductive reasoning works just fine. A new mother, a little shaky. Maybe an abusive situation she got out of when the twins were born?"

"Bree pretty much keeps to herself. I don't know that much about her."

That was both true and not true. For someone who was so amazingly gentle and tender with the babies, she seemed to have no idea whatsoever how to interact on an emotional level with other adults.

Every time he came in here and got those green eyes of hers to finally meet his, he counted it a win.

"Oh." Scott took another sip of his coffee. "I thought you two were an item. My bad."

"No, not an item. She's a friend."

And if Tanner could figure out how to get through to her, maybe so much more than that.

Chapter Twelve

When Bree stepped out the back door of the Sunrise later that evening, Tanner was waiting. He took Beth's carrier from her, leaving her with only Christian. They were almost getting too heavy for her to carry both of them in their carriers. Soon she'd need to purchase a double stroller.

There were a lot of things she'd put off purchasing, not knowing how long the twins would be hers. If Melissa was successful, it would only be a couple more weeks.

If Melissa wasn't successful… Bree had no idea what was in store for any of them.

"Thank you," she whispered to Tanner.

As they walked toward her apartment on the outskirts of town, Tanner told her about his day. Then another funny story about his family—this time about how he broke a window in his parents' house while competing with his brother, Noah, for who could twirl the baseball bat around the most times.

Tanner had won. But they'd both spent their entire spring break doing chores to pay for the window.

"How about you?" he asked. "Got any brothers or sisters?"

"No, no siblings for me. My cousin, Melissa, was the closest thing I had to a sibling."

"Did you two ever do anything stupid to get in trouble?"

Yeah, right now. The kind where they'd both be dead if the Organization found out Melissa was trying to shut them down, and Bree was not only alive, but doing whatever she could to assist Melissa.

But she just shook her head. "No, I moved away before either of us got to the rebellious age. And I've always been more of a keep-your-head-down kind of girl."

"Ah, smart. If I'd been like you, I would've gotten into a lot less trouble."

"Seems like you've done okay."

His gorgeous grin had her almost forgetting how to walk. "Depends on who you ask. Linda Dugas might say otherwise."

"Linda Dugas from the Sunday School frog incident?"

He threw back his head and laughed. "I should've known you were too smart not to remember. Yes, Linda eventually forgave me for said frog incident. She and I even dated for a few months in high school."

"It didn't work out between you two?" The thought of him with someone else shouldn't bother her at all. Who he dated in the past or might date in the future was none of her business. She refused to even acknowledge her clenching stomach.

"No. We both went off to college. She met some accountant or something, fell madly in love and moved to somewhere completely insane like Philadelphia."

She couldn't stop her own chuckle. "Philly. Yeah, man, some people just go hog wild."

"Yes! See? I knew you would understand. Why would anyone ever want to leave Colorado?"

"Why indeed?"

He nudged her with his shoulder. "How about you, anybody special in high school or college?"

She wondered what he would say if he knew she'd never finished high school, much less gone to college, but that she had an IQ higher than ninety-nine percent of the world's population.

Yet another thing that made her abnormal.

"No, I pretty much kept to myself."

Fortunately, before he could dig into that information, they arrived at the apartment. Risk Peak wasn't that big, even walking.

"Thanks for your help. You know you don't have to do this every day, right? I mean, what are the chances of something happening between here and the diner? It's probably not necessary."

She took Beth's carrier and handed him the key, as had become their habit, and waited as he checked out the tiny apartment for possible intruders. A moment later he was back. Her apartment wasn't that big.

"All clear?" she asked.

"Yep." He took Christian's carrier this time, the baby thankfully asleep, and followed her inside.

"I just feel like I'm wasting your time. I know you have a lot of responsibilities, and walking me from one safe place to another safe place down a perfectly safe street seems like a waste of taxpayers' money."

Tanner set Christian's carrier down on the table and gently unbuckled him. "Playpen?"

"Yes, please." So far, Tanner had been the only one who had the magic touch with Christian, able to soothe him and, more importantly, move him from the carrier to the playpen that served as his crib without waking him up.

Watching Tanner's big hands carry the baby so tenderly and securely, his attention entirely focused on the tiny body in his care…

Her breath caught. If Bree had ever let herself dream about what the perfect future would look like, this would've been it. A strong, gorgeous man, holding a child with such care and concern.

But these weren't her children. And he definitely wasn't her man.

And letting herself dream was only going to make all of this so much worse when she finally woke up.

Bree moved Beth into the playpen next to her brother. That little angel never made a peep, even though her big eyes blinked open once before closing again.

She closed the door to the bedroom and walked with him toward the kitchen.

"Like I was saying, it's not a good idea for you to walk me home."

He raised an eyebrow. "We've gone from 'probably not necessary' to 'not a good idea' in under a minute."

"I just…" She let out a sigh. "You've just got to have better things to do than to walk here with me every day. Dan could do it, or that other deputy…"

"Ronnie."

"Yeah, Ronnie. He could make sure I was okay." Her voice was getting a little loud and higher pitched, so she forced herself to rein it in. Why was she getting upset when making this simple request?

Tanner leaned against the wall with one shoulder and crossed his arms over his chest. His head tilted to the side as he studied her. "Do you lie when we talk, Bree?"

"What?"

He shrugged with one shoulder. "Just wondering if you tell me the truth when we talk. I know there's stuff you don't tell me, and while I don't like it, I do understand. Like today, when I asked if you have brothers or sisters and you said no, was that the truth?"

"Yes."

"So you tell me the truth when you can?"

Her eyes narrowed. "Yes. But I don't understand what you're getting at."

"Twenty-four. Teal. Strawberry. Venice. *A Wrinkle in Time*. Security gate guard. *The Matrix*."

"What?" Was he having some sort of nervous breakdown or something?

Tanner pushed off from the wall and took a step closer. "Ballerina. Dogs. And, quite unfortunately, in my opinion, pop."

She stared at him, brows furrowed. "I don't understand." It was like some sort of code that seemed familiar, but that she couldn't decipher.

"Your age. Favorite color. Favorite flavor ice cream. The city in Europe you'd most like to visit. Your favorite book as a child. The worst job ever. Best movie."

"I—"

He took another couple of steps until he was standing right in front of her. "What you wanted to be when you grew up. Which is better, dogs or cats. And favorite genre of music. Sadly."

These were the things they'd talked about on the way home from the diner each night.

"Every day I can get the answer to one question out of you. Sometimes one and a half." He reached out and tucked a strand of hair behind her ear. "I walk you here because, yes, I want to make sure you're safe. But also because each day I get to learn something about you I didn't know the day before. And that is very definitely not a waste of my time."

"Oh."

His fingers trailed down her cheek. "I know all those little things don't make up the whole of who you are. But I still want to know them. And hopefully you're learning about me as well…although not all involving frogs and Linda Dugas."

He bent down until his lips were hovering just over hers, his other hand coming up to cup her other cheek. "Walking you home is the highlight of my day. So don't try to give my job to someone else."

She was completely lost in those brown eyes. "Okay."

And then he kissed her.

His lips were soft against hers. Light, feathery brushes, but definitely different than the brief kiss of camaraderie he'd given her when they'd been hiding out in the bathroom in Denver.

When he began to nibble her lips gently, her eyes slid closed with a sigh. Her hands came up and wrapped around his wrists at her face, and she leaned into him.

But all too soon, it was over and he was pulling back, giving her a moment to regain her bearings.

"Thank you for allowing me to walk you home, Bree Daniels. I'll see you tomorrow."

And without another word, he was gone.

Chapter Thirteen

Bree wasn't even going to be able to blame the babies for her lack of sleep tomorrow. That dubious honor fell directly on Captain Tanner Dempsey's wide shoulders.

And lips.

She'd stood staring at the door for a good five minutes after he'd left, just trying to process what had happened.

Now here it was, after two o'clock in the morning, and she still was trying to understand it all. And stop replaying the feel of his lips on hers.

She'd fed the babies when they'd woken up around midnight and normally would've been fast asleep, getting as much rest as she could before they woke up again between four thirty and five.

But she wasn't. And whose fault was that?

Captain hot lips, that's who.

Why did he remember all that stuff they'd talked about over the last couple of weeks as he walked her home?

And why did that make her feel all soft and gooey in the middle?

She rolled over on her double bed and punched the

pillow next to her. When she heard something rattle against her nightstand, she thought it was from her anger management session. But then it happened again.

The phone Melissa had given her was vibrating.

Bree shot up in bed and grabbed it, opening it when she realized it was a call.

"Hello?" Her voice was tentative. She didn't want to give away any information before knowing who it was.

"Bree? Get out now!"

"Mel?"

"They found you." It was definitely Melissa. "Get the kids and get out of wherever you are. Destroy the phone. Hurry!"

"Mellie, are you safe?"

"Yes, they don't know it's me who gave you the phone, but they know it's someone from inside the Organization. I didn't realize they were tracking you already. Go now!"

Bree jumped up and pulled on her jeans and shoes. "But how will we get in touch if we don't have the phone?"

She took Beth out of the crib and rushed her to the carrier.

"I don't know. I'll be at the symposium. We'll have to find a way to get a message to each other there. We'll worry about that later. They're going to be there soon. I love you. Kiss them for me."

The phone went dead.

Bree threw the phone on the ground and stomped on it until it broke into pieces.

They had to get out now. Get to her car and leave town immediately. She refused to even think about having to leave without any sort of word to Tanner. What would he think, especially after that kiss? She forced those thoughts away or she would never make it through this.

Grabbing Beth's car seat carrier, she brought it over to the front door and set it down on the ground. Careful not to be noticed, she moved to the window and slid the curtain over just slightly so she could peek out. Her blood turned cold when she saw not one but two men walking toward her apartment in the darkness.

She darted to the back door and was pretty sure she could see someone in the darkness there.

Either door was going to spit her directly into their hands.

The only possibility would be climbing out the low kitchen window out the side of the building—maybe none of them would notice that. But the car seat carriers definitely wouldn't be an option that way.

She darted over to the bed and grabbed the baby carrier one of the ladies at the diner had lent her a couple days ago. She'd said it might help with Christian's fussiness. Bree prayed that would be the case now, because if he started howling before she made it to her car, the men would immediately be able to pinpoint her location.

She slipped the straps over her shoulder, wishing she'd paid more attention when the lady had shown her how to use it, and when it felt secure enough, she darted over to the crib and picked up Christian.

"Hey, sweet baby boy. Bree needs you to be nice and quiet, okay?"

Christian, of course, immediately began to fuss as

she lifted him, but thankfully he settled back down when he was tucked up warm against her with the carrier.

"That a boy," she murmured kissing the top of his head.

She ran over to Beth and unhooked her from the car seat. "I'm counting on you to be your normal sweet self, baby."

Bree didn't know what she was going to do when she got them to the car without their car seats, but that was the least of her worries.

Taking Beth in one arm, she pried the window open as quietly as possible. When she heard someone try the doorknob on her front door, she knew she was out of time. Abandoning all attempts at quiet, she began trying to fit herself through the large window while carrying two babies.

Getting through from the inside was easy, but there were bushes on the outside. As she heard the doorknob rattle again, she propelled herself through the window, twisting to land on her back in the bushes, protecting Beth and Christian. She swallowed a cry of pain as something sharp ripped into her shoulder, but immediately got up as best she could with arms full of babies. She heard the men, now inside her apartment, say something to each other and knew it was just a matter of seconds before they figured out where she'd gone.

She sprinted toward her car, wincing at the pain in her shoulder, afraid she might run into the third man at any moment. Deciding on stealth rather than speed, she slowed down and tucked herself into the shadows. She sucked in her breath silently when the third man passed by not ten feet away from her. He was watching the streets, obviously the lookout guy.

His phone rang, and he answered it, turning his back to her.

"What?"

She was too far away to hear what the other person said, but whatever it was, this guy wasn't happy about it.

"Well, she damn well didn't come through here. Are we sure she was even in the house in the first place?" He muttered a curse and began walking away from her, toward the front of her apartment.

It was the break Bree needed. As soon as he was far enough that it was relatively safe, she began jogging toward the car. If she could just make it there, they would be okay.

But that was when sweet, angelic Beth decided she wasn't happy with all the sleep interruptions and let out a wail.

"Oh, no, sweetie," Bree crooned, slowing to bring Beth up to her shoulder and pat her.

But that just caused Christian to start crying.

There was no way the guy on the phone didn't hear them. Forgetting about stealth, Bree bolted into a sprint, grimacing when she realized the third man was between her and her car. For the first time, Bree wished her apartment wasn't on the outskirts of town, away from everything else. Even if she started yelling, no one would hear her.

Why hadn't she called for help rather than destroy her phone? Not that anyone could've gotten here in time.

Both babies were crying now, and she was way too

slow to get away with the added weight. She glanced behind her and saw the third man was just a few feet away.

He was going to catch her. She wasn't going to make it. She pushed for one last burst of speed, but it wasn't enough.

When she felt fingers grasp at her shoulders and slip away, she started yelling. She was still too far out for anyone to hear her, but she had to try.

"Help me! Somebody help me!"

Both babies startled at her yell and wailed louder. Hard fingers gripped her shoulder, this time not letting go. Bree cried out as he jerked her back, fear coursing through her system.

The voice came heavy and dark in her ear. "You're going to regret making me chase you."

She pulled away from him, but he grabbed her hair, yanking her back. Bree struggled to hold on to the twins. And knew she couldn't allow herself to pitch forward—she might crush them.

Beth gripped firmly with one arm, Bree swung around, keeping her elbow out to use her momentum and catch the man off guard. But he was too quick and stopped her elbow before it could do any damage. He twisted her arm in a painful grip.

She got her first look at her attacker. He didn't look like a criminal. His face was nondescript, friendly even. Bree had no doubt he was from the Organization. They would send people who blended in.

His features might be neutral, but the menace in his eyes was obvious. "I'm going to enjoy teaching you some manners. And I know I'm not the only one. You've been making us look bad."

His hand raised in a fist, and she braced herself to take the punch without dropping the babies, but before he could connect, the guy went flying onto the ground.

Someone had tackled him.

Bree didn't know who it was, whether it was friend or foe or if karma had just chosen that moment to show up. She wasn't going to wait around to find out.

She took off toward the main part of town. If she could just make it another couple of blocks, she'd be able to yell for help. When someone rushed out from between two parked cars, she screamed and twisted away, trying to head in the other direction, but arms wrapped around her and held her firm.

"Bree! Bree, it's me." Tanner's voice finally got through to her. And she stopped trying to fight him.

"T-Tanner?"

"Yeah, sweetheart, it's me. Are you okay? I got a call that you were in trouble." He pulled her sideways against him, mindful of the babies, then took a crying Beth out of her arms.

"Somebody broke into my apartment. Three guys."

Tanner muttered a curse under his breath. Keeping Beth secure in one arm, he reached down and grabbed the police walkie-talkie at his belt.

"Ronnie, we've got a 10-64 off Lincoln Street. Three guys broke into Bree's apartment."

The other deputy responded, but Bree couldn't hear over the sound of her own labored breathing and the cries of the babies. When Tanner wrapped his arm back around her and began leading her somewhere, she just went.

"They found us," she said, almost on autopilot. "I've got to leave. We're not safe. They found us. They found us."

Bree could feel the panic welling up inside her. She had nothing she needed for the babies, no way of knowing if she could even get back to her car safely, and she still didn't have enough money to survive long on her own. How was she going to make it?

The world was starting to spin, the dark sky closing in on her. How was she going to do this? How would she keep the twins fed if she was on the run? Where else was going to allow her to work while good people helped look after them?

It would never happen. She wouldn't make it. What was she going to do?

Her throat was closing up, and she couldn't breathe. She began to scratch at it frantically, trying to get oxygen into her system.

Then suddenly Tanner's face was right in front of hers. His hand wrapped around the back of her head, his fingers digging into her hair. It wasn't painful, but there was definitely no ignoring it.

"Bree. Listen to me. I am not going to let anything happen to you. Not to you or the kids." As she stared into his brown eyes, so serious and authoritative, she couldn't help but believe him. Her throat loosened enough to let in some air.

"You're not in this alone anymore." His fingers rubbed at the back of her neck. "*Not alone.* Got it?"

She could only stare, couldn't quite formulate words. So Tanner moved her head in a nodding motion.

"You're going to stay here at the diner with Dan and Cheryl until I get back."

She realized she could see him so well because they'd made it back to the Sunrise. A few moments later, Cheryl and Dan pulled up in their car. Cheryl took Beth from Tanner, and Dan wrapped an arm around Bree.

Tanner reached over and kissed her forehead. "Not. Alone. Okay?"

He waited until she nodded, this time of her own accord, then took off running into the night.

Chapter Fourteen

Making sure Bree and the kids were safe had been the right priority, but damn if Tanner hadn't wanted to go straight to her apartment. Find those bastards who had put the normally reserved Bree into such a panic.

Even worse, if he hadn't received a message on his personal phone from an unknown number about the situation, he never would've been there to help her in the first place.

A three-man team? It definitely wasn't a burglary. There was nothing worth taking in an apartment that size.

When Tanner arrived back near the outside of Bree's place, Ronnie was cuffing a man.

Bree's creepy, thin guy. He was bleeding from a wound near his mouth and looked like the sleeve of his shirt had been torn.

"You read him his rights?" he asked Ronnie.

"Yep. Guy hasn't said a word."

Tanner got up in his face. "Where are your other two friends? Are they still around?"

The man just stared. "I'm not the person you're looking for. But yes, I would assume those three men are still nearby. Although what they're looking for isn't in reach, so they probably won't make themselves known."

"Oh, yeah?" Ronnie pushed the guy a little forward toward the police vehicle. "What exactly are they looking for? Bree doesn't have much cash or anything of value."

Tanner already knew what the men had been looking for. They'd been here to take Bree and the kids.

"Do you work for the people after her?" Tanner asked.

The guy looked surprised for a split second before covering it. "Believe me, I hate them more than anyone."

"What are we talking about?" Ronnie asked.

Tanner ignored his colleague. "Are you the one who sent me the message?"

"What message?" Ronnie asked, louder this time. But the man didn't respond.

Tanner turned to Ronnie. "Take him to holding then meet me back here to process the scene."

Tanner waited to see if the guy would protest his innocence or demand to be set free, but he didn't. Just silently watched what was happening around him, taking in everything.

The same way he'd been watching Bree.

Ronnie took him to the squad car, and Tanner walked the rest of the way inside the apartment, weapon drawn. He looked around her living room. Nothing seemed out of place or broken, except Bree's phone in pieces on the floor.

Once Tanner checked any place someone might be hiding and confirmed the apartment was empty, he put away his weapon. The broken phone caught his attention again. Had the burglars done that? Bree wouldn't have. She still carried that thing around with her faithfully every day.

A tap on the door had him looking up and his hand moving toward his weapon again. But it was only Scott, looking flushed and out of breath. He'd definitely been running.

"You okay?" Tanner asked.

Scott nodded. "I heard about the break-in over the walkie. Since I was awake, I thought I would come on over from the hotel, and saw a couple of guys running off one of the side streets. I followed but I wasn't able to catch them."

"Were you able to catch any sort of identifying features?"

The younger man grimaced. "No, nothing. I'm sorry."

Tanner nodded, but that wasn't the most important thing. "Next time you see something like that, be sure to call it in. You're not here to work active cases, Watson. I don't want you to get hurt."

"Will do. And maybe this is the motivation I need to get myself in better shape." Scott gave a half smile and hiked up his jeans.

It wasn't that he was really so heavy—it was more that he was cumbersome and bulky. Definitely not light or quick on his feet.

"I see you're carrying," Tanner said when he saw the holster at Scott's waist. "That's good."

The younger man touched his weapon softly. "Yeah. Always."

Tanner nodded. Maybe there was hope for this kid

to be more than just a paper pusher, if he really wanted to improve his skill sets.

"Can I help since I'm here?"

"Sure." Tanner gestured for him to come in.

Scott entered the rest of the way. "This is Bree's apartment, right? Is it a burglary?"

"If they were looking for anything valuable, she certainly doesn't have much outside of baby equipment."

Scott glanced around. "Where is she now? Is she all right?"

"Shaken up, but she's all right. She's with some friends."

And as soon as Tanner was finished here, he was going to make sure Bree and the kids went someplace safe.

Scott looked around more. "I see that kitchen window open. Did she have to climb out that? And why is her phone in pieces on the floor?"

Tanner went over to check out the open window. "Bree said there were three guys. Maybe they'd had both the front and back door covered and this was her only way out."

Fury pooled in his gut at the thought of her trying to make it out this window with both babies. She would've had to land hard and was probably more hurt than he thought. Might need medical attention. "Damn it."

Scott studied the window. "She had to have been pretty scared to go out that way with both kids in tow. Do you think the burglars made it all the way into the house?"

Tanner shook his head. "I don't think this was a burglary at all. I think it was an attempted abduction, and Bree foiled their plans by escaping."

Scott whistled through his teeth. "Abduction? To what end? Human trafficking? Selling her and the kids on the black market or something?"

Tanner wasn't going to drag Scott into the situation with Bree. Not until he had all the details. "Maybe. I plan to dig deeper into it."

"Look, man, I've got nothing but respect for you and your department here. But it's obvious you care about this woman, despite what you said earlier."

"Yeah, so?"

Scott shrugged. "Don't kill the messenger here, okay? I'm just saying if it was anyone else that maybe you weren't so attracted to, might you be considering some other…possibilities?"

"Other possibilities like what? That she's making this up?"

"No, not necessarily that. But you're right." Scott gestured around the apartment. "Nobody would break into this tiny little apartment to steal. And my kidnapping theory is pretty far-fetched, too. But what if she knew the guys who were after her?"

"Like the mob." Tanner had to admit, it did make sense. Who were these people after Bree and her cousin?

"She's new in town, right? She shows up here with her babies, needing help." Scott gave a one-shouldered shrug with a grimace. "And look, I'm not saying she doesn't need help. I'm not saying she's a criminal. But maybe these three guys who showed up tonight are people she owes money to or something. Maybe she's not completely innocent, and you should bring her in and question her officially."

Ronnie's voice spoke up from the door. "Okay, got our guy back to the station."

Scott looked surprised. "You caught one of the people who broke in?"

Tanner shook his head. "No. Just someone who happened to be out for a walk and heard some ruckus. Came to investigate. We brought him in for questioning."

Until Tanner had a chance to talk to creepy guy and ask him how the hell he knew those men were about to hit Bree's house, he didn't want to share too much information with anyone.

"He finally admitted the bumps and bruises on him were because he jumped on one of the men involved." Ronnie looked around. "Said the guy was about to hurt Bree and he couldn't let that happen."

"Lucky he was wandering around," Scott murmured.

Tanner didn't respond. It was both lucky and highly suspicious. Maybe he was the one who had been about to hurt Bree.

Bree had always seemed so skittish of the man. Was it possible she knew him and had been lying all this time? And if creepy man knew her and wanted to warn her trouble was coming, why message Tanner? Why not just contact Bree himself? He'd obviously been close by.

Too many questions. Not enough answers.

Tanner crouched down to look at the broken phone again. He was missing something big here.

"Look at it," Scott said. "That's more damage than just happens from a phone falling from your hand. Somebody stomped on it."

Scott was right. That was what Tanner had missed. The phone wasn't just broken, it was *destroyed.*

Why? And by whom?

Ronnie was still at the door. "This jamb was shimmied, but it probably wouldn't have been very loud, Tanner. How would Bree have gotten up and gotten both babies out a window in the time it took someone to break the lock and get in here? Seems impossible."

He had to agree. "Someone called and warned her."

Again, too many questions. Not enough answers.

Ronnie tilted his head and studied the pieces of the phone. "If so, it certainly seemed to make Bree mad."

"She thought someone was using the phone to trace her whereabouts," Tanner said. It made sense, given her paranoia about phones in Denver.

"This definitely goes back to her being involved with something bigger. Something she may not be admitting to," Scott said. "You really might want to question her and find out what she's been hiding. And if she's innocent, protective custody may be the safest place for her and the kids if someone from the mob is after her."

Maybe that was true, but Tanner wasn't bringing her into the station until they figured out exactly how creepy guy fit into this.

But he would send Ronnie over to the Sunrise, not only to make sure Bree was safe, but also to make sure she didn't make a run for it. Scott's comments had Tanner wondering if maybe he'd let himself be blinded to the truth. Maybe Bree wasn't a completely innocent party in all this.

Maybe he'd only been seeing what he wanted to see.

Chapter Fifteen

Creepy, thin guy's name was Bill Steele.

Two hours after leaving Bree's apartment, Tanner stared at the printout of the man's background check. Nothing unusual. An out-of-state permanent address, tax filings for the last five years and a normal employment history.

There was no indication of any criminal wrongdoing whatsoever. No warrants out for his arrest or anything suspicious. In other words, he was clean. The last time Tanner had seen a record this clean was when he'd run Bree.

An interesting coincidence.

Tanner opened the door to the interrogation room. He wanted answers.

"Mr. Steele." He took a seat across from the man. "I understand you've refused your right to counsel." Tanner hated to remind him that he could call for a lawyer, but Miranda rights weren't something to be messed with.

Steele was sitting straight in the chair, with no signs of fatigue even though it was now dawn and he'd been here for hours. He nodded briefly at Tanner's statement but didn't respond.

He obviously wasn't going to be like some suspects who immediately spilled their guts when questioned.

"Your record shows you're from Texas. That you've worked multiple construction jobs over the years. Why don't we start with how you ended up in Risk Peak?"

Steele shrugged. "I go where the work is."

"You're a long way from home. It's hard to believe there weren't any other jobs between here and Texas."

Steele's eyes were steady. "I like the mountains."

"So do I. But I have to say, if I hadn't been born and raised in Risk Peak, I'm not sure I ever would've found myself here." He leaned his forearms on the table. "According to Denny Hyde, the construction foreman, you've been here for exactly twenty-nine days."

"That sounds about right."

"Me and Denny's brother went to high school together, so we know each other pretty well. Denny was a little miffed at me because I had to wake him up in the middle of the night to ask him questions about you."

Steele crossed his arms over his chest. "And what did your good buddy Denny have to say about me?"

Tanner straightened in his chair, cocking his head to the side. "Said you show up for work every day, do your job and haven't given him a bit of trouble."

The other man raised an eyebrow. "Then there you go."

"You know what I find interesting? The fact that Denny started hiring for this project twelve weeks ago, but you didn't come on then. You came on exactly twenty-nine days ago."

"And why is that a problem?"

Now Tanner crossed his arms over his chest. He was larger than this man. Definitely heavier. But Steele wasn't intimidated by him. Tanner had sat across the interrogation table from a number of suspects who weren't intimidated by him. Some of them because of their own shape or size, some of them because they underestimated Tanner's good-naturedness and took it for weakness, and some because they were just flat-out braggarts.

But Bill Steele's lack of intimidation was something different. Like the man had already seen hell and knew there was nothing Tanner was going to do to him that could be as bad as what he'd already been through.

Steele might be a creepy, thin man, but that didn't mean he wasn't dangerous. Deadly, even.

Maybe Tanner had even underestimated *him*. He'd assumed that because of the man's gaunt face and slender build maybe he was a drug user.

But the eyes looking across from him now were not those of a man who would let narcotics control him. The thinness of his frame didn't seem to rest naturally on him. It was more like he was in recovery. But recovering from what?

"It's a problem because it was exactly one day after Bree and the twins got here."

Steele's eyes shifted away for just a second. "Coincidence."

Tanner leaned back a little farther in his chair. "You know, I might have believed that if I hadn't gotten the message from you tonight letting me know that Bree was in trouble. How did you know that?"

Steele shrugged. "I saw the guys headed toward her apartment. It's sort of isolated. I knew she was there alone with those kids and thought the guys might be looking for trouble. Ends up I was right."

"How do you know they were going to *her* apartment? If you called me when they were at her front door, there's no way I would've gotten there in time."

Steele's jaw stiffened. "Look, Dempsey, I don't sleep well. I was out for a walk, saw some guys who looked like trouble and did my civic duty. Nothing more or less than that."

"Any reason why you didn't just call 911?"

Steele's eyes shifted away again. "I guess I just had your number for some reason."

"It is public, so I guess that's a possibility." Tanner took out his phone—his piece-of-junk flip phone—and laid it on the table. "It wouldn't have anything to do with the fact that I carry this type of phone, would it?"

Steele's lips pursed and eyes narrowed. "What do you know?"

"What do *you* know?"

They stared each other down.

Steele finally shook his head, withdrawing into himself. "Nothing. I'm just a construction worker who gets to work outside with a hell of a view every day. Just counting my blessings."

Tanner didn't buy that horse manure for a second. "How did you know those men were coming for Bree?" he asked again.

But Steele wasn't budging. "Like I said, I saw them, and they gave me a hinky feeling."

Tanner decided to try a new line of questioning.

"Deputy Kitchens said you tackled one of them? That's how you got banged up."

He shrugged. "Yeah, the guy was running after Bree. Least I could do was help out."

"How do I know *you* weren't the one chasing after Bree? You've certainly been making her uncomfortable for the last couple weeks. She says you're watching her all the time."

Steele sat up straighter. "If I was trying to hurt her, there were other times that would've been a damn sight more convenient than right after I just messaged you and told you she needed help."

That, Tanner believed. He didn't think Steele had been one of the guys after Bree. But he did think the man wanted something from her. Maybe Scott was right. Maybe Bree owed somebody money and this was about collecting.

"Did you know Bree before you came here, Steele?"

"I can promise you I had never heard of Bree Daniels before I set foot in Risk Peak." Frustration grew inside Tanner. He didn't think Steele was actually lying to him, he just wasn't telling the whole truth.

Exactly how he often felt about Bree.

It was like the answers were right there in front of him, if he just knew what questions to ask.

"Are you or Bree involved with the mob? Does she owe someone money? Does it have something to do with the same people her cousin is mixed up with?" Tanner felt like he was throwing spaghetti against the wall, hoping something would stick.

"Mob? No. Money? I don't think so. And I have no

idea who Bree is, truly, so I don't know who her cousin or any other family is."

"Melissa Weathers."

If he hadn't been watching Steele so closely, he never would've seen it. Hell, he was looking directly at the man and almost didn't see it. Steele didn't startle, didn't stiffen, but the air around him changed.

He knew Melissa.

Tanner leaned forward until he was nearly halfway over the narrow table. "You know Melissa, don't you? Do you work for the people Melissa works for? Do you know what they're up to? How to stop them?"

Whatever Steele had been feeling, he swallowed it fast. "I don't work for anybody but Denny Hyde. And you know what? I'm tired. Either charge me and I'll call an attorney, or I'm ready to go. You can't hold me."

It was true. And although they could hold him for a few more hours, if he was requesting counsel, he would be out of here in no time.

"We're not going to charge you." Tanner made one last appeal. "But tell me what's going on so I can help. I can't protect Bree if I don't know what I'm up against."

Steele stood, and Tanner thought he would leave without saying anything else, but when he got to the door, he turned back. "Get her—get *them*—out of here. Out of this town, where no one can find them. Do it right now. Don't wait."

That was exactly what he'd planned on doing.

"Why? Who's coming, Steele?"

"Someone way too big for you to fight. Just get them out while you can."

He was gone without another word.

Chapter Sixteen

Bree had to get out. Out of Risk Peak, out of the entire state of Colorado.

She was currently inside Cheryl and Dan's office. Both babies were asleep—completely unharmed, thank God—in the playpen Cheryl and Dan had set up weeks ago.

Bree tried to think through the panic that seemed to surround her like a haze. The Organization had found her. If she stayed here any longer, she'd be putting everyone in danger. Herself. The babies. The Andrewses. Tanner.

Tanner. He'd gone running back toward the danger hours ago, and she hadn't heard from him. He'd thought he was dealing with a run-of-the-mill break-in, when the Organization was so much more dangerous than that. They wouldn't hesitate to kill him if it suited their purposes.

She paced back and forth across the office like she had dozens of times already tonight.

Was Tanner hurt? She should've told him more, done what she could to prepare him for what he would be up against, rather than send him in blind thinking he was just dealing with some burglars. She opened the door to the office, even knowing she would be too late to help him. She had to try.

Cheryl and Dan were sitting, bleary-eyed, at the booth closest to the kitchen, sipping coffee. Deputy Ronnie was at the counter, pouring himself a cup. She hadn't even realized he was here.

"I need to go help Tanner. He might be in danger."

Ronnie shook his head. "Nobody was at your place by the time we got there. They must've gotten spooked."

"And nobody was hurt? Tanner is all right?"

Ronnie nodded. "Yep. He's at the station now questioning a suspect. He wanted me to stay here and make sure you…" He trailed off.

"Make sure Bree and the kids were safe?" Cheryl finished for him.

Ronnie looked a little sheepish. "Yeah. Make sure they were safe."

But that was obviously not what he'd intended to say.

"Who's the suspect Tanner is questioning?" Dan asked.

Ronnie took a sip of his coffee and rubbed the back of his neck. "Come on now, Mr. A. You know I can't talk about that sort of stuff."

"Is it somebody from around here? It must be someone we know if you're keeping his identity a secret," Cheryl argued. "We just want to make sure Bree is safe. Why don't you just give us a little information while I make you some breakfast, Ronnie. You look hungry."

Watching the middle-aged man be so skillfully manipulated would've been entertaining to Bree if she wasn't so desperate to hear who was being questioned.

"I definitely wouldn't say no to some of your pancakes, Mrs. A. And honestly, I don't know the guy's name. Truly." He raised an eyebrow. "Although I will say he could definitely use some of your cooking."

Dan's and Cheryl's eyes flew to Bree's.

Creepy, thin man.

Damn it, she'd known he was watching her. She didn't know why he'd waited so long to make his move—maybe he'd been trying to confirm her identity before he did anything. It didn't matter, and it didn't matter that Tanner had arrested him. The Organization would get him out almost immediately, or they would just send someone else to come after her.

Bree had to leave *now.*

Without another word, she spun back toward the kitchen and the office.

She was grabbing everything that had accumulated in here over the past few weeks. The room looked less like an office and more like a day care. Bree's heart clenched. Cheryl and Dan had changed so much of their lives to make room for her and the babies. And now Bree had to run.

She was stuffing diapers everywhere she could—not unlike what she'd been doing when she first showed up in Risk Peak—when Cheryl appeared in the doorway. "I've tried my best not to ask you questions you might not want to answer. I know those children aren't yours, but I know you love them and want what's best for them."

Bree tried to swallow past the lump in her throat. She knew she wouldn't be able to get words out, so she just nodded.

"I know you think you need to run, but why don't you stay? Let us help. Me, Dan, Tanner—hell, most of Risk Peak would fight for you and them kids. Whoever your creepy guy is, or whoever decides to come after you, we can face them together."

Now Bree couldn't stop the tears from overflowing. "I can't stay."

She could elaborate more, spin up some tale of partial truths, but the fact was the Organization knew she was here. If she stayed, the town might fight for her, but the Organization would win and take Bree and the babies anyway. The best she could do for these people she'd started to care about—the first community she'd ever known—was to get out.

She started packing stuff up again.

"We don't want you to go." The voice from the door this time was Dan's.

A little sob escaped Bree before she could swallow it. She took a couple of deep breaths to get herself under control.

Where was all the training her mother had spent years instilling in her? Now Bree understood why the no-friendship rule had been so important. Because leaving friends without a backward glance was not an easy thing to do.

"Just for a few days until things calm down, then I'll be back," Bree finally said. That was a lie. She would never be coming back to Risk Peak again.

She heard Dan and Cheryl whispering to each other in the doorway. Were they going to try to talk her out of this? She couldn't let them. She just needed to get out while she still had the resolve to do so.

Once she had everything she could fit into the large diaper bag, she reached down to grab the babies.

She was putting Christian inside the baby carrier when Dan walked back into the room. She hadn't even realized he left. He set two baby car seat carriers on the ground. "We bought those a couple of days ago thinking it might be easier to have two sets than to have to lug them back and forth all the time."

Bree had no idea what to say. "I—I…"

Cheryl walked over and took Christian from her, kissing him on the head. "If you've got to go, then you've got to go. Your apartment might still be closed off as a crime scene. But at least you'll have car seats."

"Thank you." The simple thanks was so completely inadequate, but it was all Bree could think of. The older couple fastened the babies inside the car seats with the utmost care. Bree gathered the rest of the stuff.

"We want you to have this." Dan pressed something into her hand, and when she looked down she realized it was a wad of cash.

She shook her head vehemently. "No. I can't take this."

Dan closed one of his hands over hers with the cash. "You can, and you will. Cheryl and I both agree there's nothing more important to us—nothing we could spend this money on—that would make us more happy than knowing that you and those children are safe. So you take it and maybe that will give you even more reason to come back around when you can."

She had to get out of here. Her mom had been right. No closeness was worth the agony she was feeling now. And Dan and Cheryl weren't even Tanner. Thank God she didn't have to say goodbye to him. She didn't think she would survive it.

But when they walked out to the front of the restaurant, there Tanner was standing in the doorway.

Staring at him, his dark hair tousled and brown eyes tired, she knew she didn't have the strength to fight him if he asked her to stay. Not even if it was what was best for him or her.

But those words weren't what came out of his mouth.

"You running?" Those strong arms crossed over his massive chest.

"I… Yes. It's what's best."

He nodded and definitely didn't look surprised. "Fine. I'll give you a police escort to the county line."

Almost from a distance, she heard Cheryl gasp and Dan say Tanner's name sharply, but he didn't respond and she found she couldn't look away from his brown eyes.

Eyes that had been so warm earlier tonight when he'd walked her home but were coldly focused now.

He'd finally realized what she'd known all along. She was trouble for this town, and having her here was a mistake.

THE WALK TO her car was made in silence. What could be said anyway? This was what she wanted, right?

He took the babies in their new carriers. "I'll put them in the car. Get whatever else you need from your apartment. It doesn't look like there was any damage to anything."

Was that what this was about? Did he think she'd made the whole thing up or something?

It didn't matter. It didn't matter that her legs were as heavy as her heart as she walked through her apartment door. It didn't matter that she had no plan. Had let herself become complacent and now would be paying the price.

It didn't matter that she was so weary that she just wanted to lie down on the floor and cry.

Not an option.

She looked over to the spot where she'd crushed the phone. It was gone now. She didn't know if Tanner had taken it for evidence or if the men who broke in had picked up the pieces.

She gathered the twins' items and anything she would be able to fit in her car, and made her way back outside.

Tanner was crouched down by the back seat, murmuring something to one of the babies, but he straightened when she came back out. He took the stuff from her and placed it in her trunk without saying a word.

"I'm sorry I brought trouble into your town," she finally said as she got behind the wheel. She was just trying to hold it together until she got away from him. There would be nothing but time to fall apart once she was on the go.

"I'm sorry this happened, too, Bree. Don't stop driving until you're completely out of town. Straight out Highway 70. Good luck."

Without another word, he shut her door and turned away.

And that was it. She started the car and pulled away from the curb. By the time she'd made it out of Risk Peak, tears were stinging her eyes. She kept driving out

Highway 70 like Tanner had told her. Why not? She didn't have any better plan.

A few miles out of town, there was some sort of detour, and she had to turn off on a side road. She thought nothing about it until she'd gone a half mile and there was a large car parked horizontally, blocking the road in front of her and forcing her to slow.

Fear trickled down her spine. Had she literally just driven into a trap set by the Organization? She'd been so caught up in her own personal drama she hadn't been paying attention. Maybe they'd been counting on that.

When two men got out of the car in front of her, she slammed on the brakes. She was just about to throw her car in Reverse when an SUV pulled up behind her, boxing her in.

Even though the temperature in the car was comfortable, sweat coated her body. With her own stupidity, she'd gotten them caught not even two miles out of town. Frantically, she tried to think of what she could do. If she ran, would they follow her? Leave the babies alone? But then what if nobody found them in time?

Her stomach was cramping in panic. She tried to think of what her mother would've done in the same situation.

Her mother never would've gotten herself in this situation. She would've left the babies at the first homeless shelter she could find an hour after they'd shown up in her car.

A tap on the window startled a scream out of Bree. She looked out the windshield first and saw two large men moving toward her, then looked out her window to see who had knocked, fearing the worst.

Chapter Seventeen

Tanner felt like a complete heel as he knocked on Bree's window. She had no color left in her face and was looking like she might vomit at any second. He hated that he had put her through this, but there'd been no other way. Her car had the tracking device and a transmitter.

She was looking at him, sucking in deep breaths, confusion clear on her face. Tanner put his finger up to his lips in a motion to be quiet and then gestured for her to open the door.

As soon as she did, he put two fingers over her lips, then reached over and cranked up the radio. As he helped Bree out of the car, he nodded to the two men who were assisting him—Zac Mackay and Gavin Zimmerman, friends of Tanner's brother—two men who had no tie whatsoever to Risk Peak. They went around to either side of the car and gently picked up the car seat carriers with the kids inside.

"I—" Bree started, but Tanner shook his head.

"There's both a tracking device and a recording device in your car," he whispered close to her ear. "The radio will drown out most of what we say, but not all."

If anything, her face got even paler. She nodded, and

he led her over to his mother's car, a late-model Honda CR-V. They all got inside, a tight fit with four adults and two baby carriers.

"I don't understand what's happening," Bree said as soon as the doors closed.

Tanner gave her the most reassuring smile he could. "This is Gavin and Zac. They both served in the army with my brother, Noah. They live a couple hours from here in Wyoming. Gavin is going to take your car back in that direction and hopefully lead the people searching for you on a wild goose chase."

Zac gave her his charming grin that made Tanner itch to punch his friend in the face. "I'm just here as taxi service before going directly back home."

Bree looked at Gavin and Zac before returning her eyes to Tanner. "But I thought you wanted me out of Risk Peak."

"When I found the tracker and the bug, I knew you weren't safe in town anymore. But I needed to make it look like I thought it was better if you were gone. That you weren't my problem anymore and I had no idea of your whereabouts."

And he was going to catch hell for it. His phone was already ringing off the hook—friends, family, damn near everyone—and it would just continue to get worse as word spread.

"Oh. I didn't understand," Bree whispered.

As if he hadn't known that from the moment he'd mentioned leaving at the Sunrise. She was terrified and thought he'd just kicked her out on her own without so much as a goodbye.

That, they would be talking about later. Right now they had bigger problems.

"How did you know to get out of your apartment?"

"Melissa called me. They were tracking the phone. She told me to destroy it and get out."

He wanted more details, but they didn't have time.

Tanner reached over and covered Bree's hand that was clenched around the car seat. "I'm going to help hide you. But Gavin has to take your car, and you might never see it again."

"That's fine," she whispered.

"I'll get all the twins' stuff out of it first. Stay here, okay?"

She nodded, exhaustion bracketing her mouth.

Tanner got out of the car with Zac and Gavin.

"I owe you guys one." He was careful to keep his volume low enough for the transmitter not to pick it up over the radio.

Zac shook his head. "Your brother is like family to us, so that means you are, too. But those tracking and transmitting devices are high-end. She's got some big-name trouble after her, I'm afraid."

Tanner was afraid of that, too.

Gavin slapped him on the shoulder. "We'll get them off your tail for as long as possible. You're going to have your hands full. Have Noah give a shout in our direction if you need the sort of help that doesn't involve government red tape, and we'll be there."

Tanner was hoping it wouldn't come to that.

He got the rest of Bree's belongings from her car and transferred them to his. A few moments later, Bree's car was pulling away, Gavin behind the wheel, Zac following in the second car.

He didn't have to worry about Zac and Gavin—they were both former Special Forces. They knew how to surveil, mislead and adapt to changing circumstances. If anyone could trick the people after Bree, it was them.

He made his way back to the car. Bree had fastened the babies' car seats in the back seat and climbed in the front.

Fear and exhaustion still pulled at her pale skin.

"I'm sorry I had to be a jerk back in town."

She gave a nod. "It's okay. I understand."

He wasn't exactly sure what she understood. "I thought maybe you would see that I was trying to let you know something was wrong."

She shrugged. "I thought you finally wanted what was best for Risk Peak—me gone."

"Even after what happened yesterday afternoon?" He started the car.

"It was a kiss. It happens all the time."

He raised an eyebrow. "Does it happen all the time to you, Bree?"

She turned and looked out the window as he turned the SUV in the direction they needed to go. "Does it matter?"

In the greater scheme of things, with all his questions… no, it didn't really matter. But he wanted her to admit it meant something.

"Even if I had wanted you gone, I wouldn't have done it like that, Bree. Wouldn't have just told you to hit the road."

"Sometimes to do the smart thing you have to make

a hard decision. I didn't blame you for that. You have a town you're responsible for. I'm not what's important."

"How can you say that? Everybody in Risk Peak loves you."

She shrugged. "They love Christian and Beth. I'm just part of that package. If I was here by myself, no one would care as much. I wouldn't be a big deal."

"That's not true."

And she was a big deal to him. But he wasn't sure if saying so would make things better or worse.

Like some of the horses he helped Noah raise, Bree needed time and gentling. He would try to give as much as he could of both.

She didn't say anything as time ticked by, just continued to stare out the window.

"Where are we going?" she finally asked.

"My house."

"In Risk Peak? Is that a good idea?"

He took a turn that led them in the opposite direction of the way they'd ultimately be going. Probably an unnecessary step, but one he was willing to take to ensure Bree's safety.

"I have a small apartment in Risk Peak, since it's more convenient for the hours I sometimes have to keep with the job. But that's not my actual house. I own a horse ranch with my brother, Noah, about twenty miles outside town."

"Horses?" She sounded like she couldn't quite understand it.

"Yes. Noah's house is on one end of our acreage, and he does most of the daily ranch work. But that ranch is home for me. Has been for nearly ten years."

"I didn't know that."

He shrugged. "I didn't tell you. I was just going to surprise you by taking you there one day. Guess that's today. Surprise."

"Do you think anyone will try to look for us there? Maybe Cheryl and Dan?"

He grimaced. "After what I just said at the Sunrise, I don't think anyone will be searching my property for you."

Her eyes closed. "Yeah." She paused for a few moments. "Are you sure, Tanner? Are you sure you want us there? It's one thing not to run us out of town and help us. But to bring us into your home? Are you sure that's what you want?"

All her words came out in a rush, as if she was afraid she was pointing out something he hadn't considered.

No other woman had ever lived with him there. Definitely no babies. He wouldn't have made this offer to just anyone. The ranch was important to him. Sacred, even. Not something he shared lightly.

He was surprised at how much he wanted Bree there.

He glanced at her for a second before turning his eyes back to the road. "I want you there. It's the safest place for you. I'll be there to make sure everything is secure, and when I'm not, I know Noah will have an eye on you and the kids. Family are the only ones I can completely trust in a situation like this."

A situation like what? Where a woman he barely knew, but who blew his focus straight to hell every time she was around, was coming to live with him? One where he wasn't certain of the exact danger, but suspected it was way more complicated than the mob?

One where protocol said he should be taking her into protective custody right now, not taking her to his own damn house?

But thankfully she didn't ask what he meant by *situation*. She was stuck on another word.

"Family," she muttered, as if the concept was foreign to her.

"They're the only ones you can ultimately trust, right?"

She began rubbing at a spot on her shoulder. "I guess."

"You'll like Noah. He's quiet, keeps to himself. Since he got out of the Special Forces, he hasn't really wanted to be around people much."

She leaned the side of her face against the headrest and stared at eyes shadowed with exhaustion. "Sounds like a male version of me, minus the military background."

He smiled gently at her. "There's some similarities. Noah would definitely rather be around horses than people. Do you like horses?"

"I've never been around a horse before."

That didn't surprise him at all.

"But I've always wanted to be around animals or have a pet," she continued, her voice getting softer, eyes drooping. "But we never could."

"Who never could, Freckles?" He felt a little bad for fishing for info while her defenses were down and she was so exhausted. But there was one thing he was sure of: he had to solve the puzzle of Bree Daniels in order to be able to protect her.

"Me and Mom. We couldn't have pets because they would hamper us every time we had to leave suddenly."

"And how often was that?"

Bree let out a yawn. "Three or four times."

That wasn't as bad as he thought. "It must have been hard moving around three or four times in your life. Maybe a pet would've helped with your transition."

"No."

"No, it wouldn't have helped?"

Another yawn. "No, we moved three or four times a year. I never knew when. That's why I could never have a pet or friends. It was better that way for when we had to leave."

He gripped the steering wheel tighter. "Why would you need to leave so suddenly that many times?"

"If they found us, or sometimes if Mom even thought they might be close, we had to leave."

"If who found you?"

"Them. The Organization."

He glanced at her again, and her eyes were still closed. "Who is the Organization, sweetie?"

"They're the people who are going to kill us all."

He waited for her to say more, gritting his teeth when she didn't. He was about to probe her for more info when he realized she was asleep.

"Aw, hell, sweetheart."

He let her sleep. She needed rest.

A little over forty-five minutes later, sure no one was following them, Tanner pulled off onto the long driveway leading up to his house on the ranch.

He carried the twins inside. They would need a bottle soon, but hopefully he could at least move Bree inside first. Leaving the babies in his office with the door closed in case they started crying, he went back out to get Bree. The fact that she had fallen asleep at all was surprising.

The fact that she kept sleeping as he slipped his arms around her and picked her up was a testament to her exhaustion.

He'd just gotten in the door when she stirred.

"Tanner?"

"Shh," he said, easing the door closed behind him with his foot.

"The kids..." she murmured before a huge yawn overtook her.

"How about just for today you let someone take care of you. I can handle Christian and Beth."

He halfway expected an argument. But instead she snuggled into him.

Tanner pulled her closer, willing to accept her trust as what it was: a treasure.

Chapter Eighteen

Bree sat straight up in the bed, looking around. Something was wrong.

It was way too quiet, and the sun was high in the sky—probably midafternoon. When was the last time she'd woken up based on her body telling her it was time rather than because one of the twins needed something?

It took her a moment to get her bearings. She was in a giant king-size bed.

Tanner's bed.

She had no idea how to process that, so she threw off the blanket and jumped down. She was still fully dressed, except for her shoes, which sat neatly by the door. She rushed into the living room but heard no sound of either child crying.

Beth could possibly go this long without fussing. But Christian?

The house wasn't that big. She dashed into a room that seemed to be an office/library but found no signs of life. A blanket was dropped haphazardly on the sofa in the living room, but it was empty, as well were the back porch and large eat-in kitchen.

Panic truly struck at Bree. Where were the babies? How could she have just *slept* like this?

She'd worked herself into such a state that she almost missed them as she walked by the window and came to an abrupt halt, unable to believe her eyes.

Actually, she could. And that was the problem.

Tanner stood outside in the sunshine, a baby in each arm. He was bouncing them both gently, talking to them in words Bree couldn't hear and showing them the horses in the corralled area in front of them.

Beth and Christian were too young to process anything they were seeing, which Tanner had to have known, but they were looking out at the animals like they were listening intently to whatever it was Tanner was telling them.

Bree's heart gave a little flutter.

Then she realized Tanner was wearing a cowboy hat. One obviously well-worn and loved.

Then her heart gave a big flutter.

She had to remind herself that Michael Jeter and the Organization would scour the earth to find her if he knew she was alive. No ranch would save her, no matter how remote or what type of Special Forces soldier Tanner's brother had been.

She could not think of this place—think of this *man*—as permanent. Bree would only be here for a few days.

As soon as she opened the door, Tanner turned toward her and gave her a smile that stole her breath.

A few days. A few days.

"Morning." His voice was husky, soft. "Well, afternoon, actually."

"Hi," she replied, taking Christian from him.

He half turned back toward the horses. "We were talking about all the animals' names and how long they've lived here."

"Thank you for letting me sleep. Have they been fed?"

"Yep, and are dry and happy. We were outside enjoying the sunshine and meeting the animals."

Bree held her face up to the sun. When was the last time she'd just enjoyed being outside without worrying about being spotted by someone or accidentally captured on their cell phone?

Never, except for the rarest of occasions.

They walked around, Tanner pointing out different horses. A few minutes later, a large Labrador retriever came out of the tree line and began sniffing Bree.

"That's Corfu."

Bree reached down and rubbed the dog's head affectionately. "Corfu?"

"Yeah, it's a Greek isle. One of the places my brother visited when he was stationed overseas. I've always wanted to go."

She smiled. "Okay, I guess Corfu works for a pretty dog like him."

"Actually her. And she's pregnant. It won't be long until we have a slew of puppies around here." Tanner crouched down so the dog could lick his face, carefully keeping Beth to the side so the dog didn't frighten her.

Bree stared at the dog, wide-eyed. "Puppies," she murmured. "How many?"

"Usually between three and five. We'll give most

of them away to people in town. Definitely keep one around here."

Bree just nodded. No sense thinking about cute little puppies that weren't hers. Or the babies that weren't hers. Or the home that wasn't hers.

Or the man that wasn't hers.

"If Corfu is around, that means Noah will be showing up any second also."

Sure enough, a few moments later a man came riding out of the trees from the opposite direction than she'd been expecting him.

Tanner rolled his eyes. "Surveilling?" he asked his brother.

Noah shrugged and slipped from the saddle. "Can't be too careful." He turned toward her but didn't move closer. "Ma'am."

It was plain these two were definitely brothers. Both tall, broad shouldered. Same dark coloring and good looks. But where Tanner was approachable and trustworthy, Noah was closed off, wary, defensive.

She wasn't drawn to Noah at all like she was Tanner, but she definitely understood him.

"Nice to meet you," she murmured, taking a slight step back.

He gave her a brief nod before turning back to Tanner. "I've already gotten three calls from Cassandra, since you're not answering your phone, and one from Mom. Gotten quite an earful about how you ran a young mother and her twin babies out of town." He raised an eyebrow. "Doesn't look like they got far. These yours?" he asked his brother, gesturing to the babies.

"No," Tanner said, rolling his eyes.

"They're not even mine," Bree put in.

Noah tilted his head to the side and gave something that looked like a rusty smile. "You always did know how to complicate things, bro."

Tanner chuckled, but it faded quickly. "They need to lie low here for a while. Completely off the grid. No phones anywhere around."

That request didn't seem to faze Noah at all. He just nodded. "Trouble?"

Tanner nodded. "Of a big kind."

"How big?"

Tanner turned to her. "You want to provide details?"

She balanced Christian on her hip and turned to the side. "I can't. Not right now. I'm sorry, but I can't give you details." If anything went wrong, it would be signing their death warrants. Although she might have done that even if she didn't tell them.

"Makes it harder to protect you that way," Tanner said.

She swallowed the panic building up in her. "I know. Maybe I should leave. If you could lend me a car or—"

"No." Both Dempsey brothers said it at the same time.

"But I—"

Tanner moved closer until he was right in front of her. She had to crane her neck back to see him. "You're not leaving here on your own. Nobody knows you're here. You lie low like you said you needed to. We'll figure out the rest."

"Okay. But if—"

Tanner's phone beeping in his pocket cut her off. He cursed under his breath when he looked at the screen.

"I've got to get into town if we have any hope of keeping your location here a secret. Evidently I'm not very popular right now."

Bree bit her lip. "Are you going to get in trouble?"

He winked at her. "I'm sure Mrs. A is ready to snatch me out of Sunday School class again. But in the end, all that matters is your safety. They'll all forgive me after this blows over."

She grabbed his arm. "And if it's not something that ever blows over?"

"Then we take it one day at a time."

"How long do Zac and Gavin think they can buy you?" Noah asked.

Tanner shifted Beth to his other arm. "Two or three days max. Then Gavin will make it look like Bree ditched the car." He turned to her. "But if this Organization is as proficient as you say at utilizing electronics for their purposes, it won't take them long to figure out they were tricked."

She looked over at Noah. "I'm not trying to lead danger to your friends."

Noah shrugged. "They can take care of themselves."

Tanner looked over at his brother. "Call Cassandra and get her to come out here, then once she is, figure out a way for her to get whatever baby supplies the kids will need. But don't mention it over the phone."

"Will do."

"And you'll probably want to carry." Both men nodded at each other in clear understanding.

"Carry what?" Bree asked.

"His weapon. We're not going to take any chances with your life. Everybody in town knows not to come around here—Noah doesn't like company. Anybody else coming around is just looking for trouble. Cassandra, our sister, will get you anything you need."

Before Tanner could say anything else, Noah whistled at Corfu then swung up onto his horse and headed out without a word. They both watched him go.

"He doesn't talk a lot."

"I know," Tanner said. "He has his own personal demons. But he'll keep you safe. Even if you can't see him, know that if I'm not here, he's got an eye on you and the kids. Nothing's going to happen."

Someone else she was dragging into danger. The list got longer and longer. "Tanner, I—"

He put a finger over her lips. "Don't say it again. You're not leaving. I want you here. Noah wants you here, even if he can't formulate the words. You're not going off on your own."

He led her inside and gave her a brief tour of the small, charming house that was obviously dear to him. Tanner handed her Beth then reached over and kissed her forehead. "I'll be home as soon as I can. It might be a while."

A few moments later, he was walking out the door. She just stared at the door he'd shut behind him.

Home.

For the first time in her adult life she would be waiting for someone at *home*.

Chapter Nineteen

Gayle Little didn't say a word to Tanner as he walked into the department office. Gayle had been a staple in the department before Tanner's dad had been sheriff. She'd been welcoming Tanner into the building since he was about ten years old.

But not today.

Today the coffeepot was cold. It was midafternoon, so not prime coffee-drinking hours, and Tanner had never demanded or expected Gayle to make it, she just always had.

There was no fresh coffee today.

And her glare was even colder than the coffeepot.

Evidently word about him running Bree out of town had spread, which was exactly what he wanted, but it was still a little painful.

He spent the next couple of hours going through the forty-nine voice mail messages, an untold number of emails and a dozen handwritten notes telling him—some more politely than others—what they thought of his actions with Bree. He didn't dare set foot inside the Sunrise for a while. Mr. and Mrs. A were likely to poison him.

Nobody was happy.

Bree wouldn't believe it if she could see it. Wouldn't believe so many people would care about her.

That was a misconception he planned to rectify once the danger had passed, no matter how long it took. And she could just keep sleeping in his bed while they worked on it. He would take the couch as long as he needed to.

Or maybe, if he was the luckiest bastard on the planet, she might invite him to join her.

He shut down the emails and deleted the voice mails. There was nothing he could do about them right now. His office phone rang, and he cringed when he saw who it was. This call he couldn't ignore.

"What can I do for you, Sheriff Duggan?"

Blaine Duggan had been his boss since day one. She'd worked with Tanner's dad and had promoted Tanner steadily over the years. She was his mom's good friend, and he had nothing but respect for the older woman.

"You're quite the talk of the town today, Dempsey. My office is getting calls."

"Sorry, Sheriff. Guess I made an unpopular decision."

He didn't want to lie to his boss, but he wasn't sure if this call was being monitored.

"Anything I should know about?"

"Not at this time. I believe it was the right decision for my department and Risk Peak in general, and the people contacting you don't necessarily have all the facts."

"Which is exactly what I told them."

"I appreciate your trust, ma'am."

He was about to say his goodbyes when she spoke again. "But I buried your father because he got in over his head and didn't ask for help. I don't want you making the same mistakes. Take care of yourself, Tanner."

The call clicked off before he could say anything else. He stared at the phone receiver in his hand.

Was Tanner being just as blind as his father had been? He didn't think Bree would put a gun to his head, but he couldn't deny that he was courting danger by bringing her into his house.

But he still meant what he'd told her. He wasn't leaving her to deal with this alone.

He spent the next hour fielding calls he wished he could send straight to voice mail and looking over the report from the break-in to make sure there was nothing he'd missed.

Nobody in the office was talking to him. Gayle still wouldn't even look at him, so that at least allowed him to get a little more work done. He sent Ronnie to pick up Bill Steele from the construction site.

Tanner wanted to talk to him again. Maybe the man would refuse to come in. He certainly had that right. But Tanner wanted to see the man's face when he mentioned the *Organization*. The term was vague and obviously an inside reference, but Tanner was willing to bet Steele was familiar with it.

Tanner wanted a name. A real name. He didn't think Steele was working for said Organization, but maybe he had some details that would help Tanner better protect Bree and the kids.

And like it or not, she was going to have to tell him everything she knew.

Because there were puzzle pieces that didn't fit. Like if the Organization was the current threat, the people *who were going to kill them all*, according to her, then why had she and her mother been running from them when Bree was a child?

And if she hadn't seen her cousin in a decade, why were the same people who'd been after Bree's mom now after her cousin?

First he would find out what Steele knew, then he would use it to frame all the questions he had for Bree.

A tap on his door a few minutes later had Tanner looking up from his desk with a cringe. Was someone else here to tell him what a terrible person he was?

Scott stuck his head in. "Hey, boss. I brought you a sandwich from the Sunrise."

"Did you tell them it was for me?"

"No. Should I have? Do they do something special for your sandwiches?"

Tanner let out a sigh. "No. They just probably would've spit in it—or worse—if they'd known it was for me."

"Because of the whole Bree situation?"

He scrubbed a hand across his jaw. He needed a shave. "I guess you heard?"

Scott's baby face scrunched up. "The way the people around here are telling it, you lit her on fire before escorting her out of town."

Tanner rolled his eyes and took the sandwich Scott offered. "Got to love small-town drama. Bree told me she was leaving, and I didn't try to stop her. Like you said, I think she might be caught up with the mob or a gang or something. While I feel bad for her, really, my overall priority has to be to the town."

"So you're just going to leave the whole break-in alone? That doesn't seem right."

Good for you, kid. Hold the line. "No, you're right. I don't care who it is, someone breaking into a house isn't okay here. We've got forensics seeing if they can pick up any prints, but it doesn't look hopeful."

"Didn't Ronnie say you had a suspect? Anything come of that?"

"It was Bill Steele, that guy who was making Bree nervous. But we didn't have enough to charge him." Tanner gestured to the chair in front of his desk. "Want to come in?"

"Do you think Steele is one of the men who broke into her apartment?" Scott sat down as Tanner began unwrapping the sandwich.

"Maybe. I've got some more questions I'd like to ask him. Ronnie has gone to bring him back. Hopefully he'll come voluntarily, because we definitely don't have enough to charge him."

But maybe he would want to go. Maybe, like Bree, Steele was concerned about phones tracking his location.

Fine. If he wouldn't—or felt like he couldn't—come to the department, Tanner would go out and find him. Steele didn't have to give him answers in an official setting, but he had to give Tanner some answers. It could be in the middle of a field as far as Tanner was concerned.

"Would you mind if I sat in on the questioning? See if I can learn something?"

"Yeah, we'll see." On one hand, the kid was pretty

observant and might see or hear things Tanner missed. On the other hand, Steele was already pretty closed off. Having other people around wasn't going to help the man feel free to speak.

Tanner was one bite into his sandwich when his office phone rang.

"Tanner Dempsey."

"It's Ronnie. We've got a problem. Steele didn't show up for work today."

"Did he call in sick? We know for a fact he was up all night."

"Nope," Ronnie said. "Just didn't show up at all. I got his address from Denny Hyde and went over to the place he's renting. He's gone, Tanner."

"What?" Tanner stood, sandwich forgotten.

"Yep. He was renting Sue Ragan's place that she made out of her barn. And by the looks of it, he lit out of here in a hurry. You need to get here right away."

"Why?"

"We definitely should've arrested Steele while we had the chance."

Chapter Twenty

Mrs. Ragan's house was a couple of miles outside town, so Tanner drove, Scott riding with him, since the younger man looked so crestfallen at being left behind.

As soon as Tanner walked into the room where Steele had been staying, he let out a string of curses that would've made a seasoned sailor proud.

Steele had played him.

The walls were covered in photos of Bree and the babies. Dozens of them. He'd definitely been watching her—*stalking her*—since the day he arrived.

There were pictures of her at work, her walking home, her with Tanner, her taking a break at the back of the Sunrise. Worse, there were just as many pictures of the babies as there were of Bree.

"Nobody touch anything," Tanner said as he donned a pair of gloves and walked inside. "Ronnie, get the crime lab over here ASAP."

Ronnie was already calling it in when Tanner found a handwritten note listing Bree and the kids' schedule and habits.

Bree had been right to be wary of the creepy, thin man. This was nothing less than obsession.

And Tanner had had the man in custody and chose to let him go. He'd clung to a more complicated scenario—that Steele had known or been a part of some sort of hidden nefarious organization—rather than the simple one that was undoubtedly true: Steele was fixated on Bree and the kids.

And now wished he could kick his own ass.

Had everything Steele said this morning been a lie? And why had he called Tanner last night when Bree had been in trouble? *Before* Bree had really been in trouble?

"County forensics team is on their way, Tanner." Ronnie came back in the room. "I spoke to Mrs. Ragan—she said Steele is paid up through the end of the month and she's never had a problem with him. She heard him squeal out of here early this morning."

"Did she notice which direction he was going?"

"Away from town. North up Highway 70."

So the same direction Gavin was driving Bree's car. Was Steele the one who had put the tracker on it? Had the whole break-in at her house been a setup to get her to run scared?

"Wow." Scott whistled through his teeth. "This is some pretty advanced-level stalker stuff. Are we sure he isn't Bree's baby daddy?"

"No, he wasn't. She would've mentioned that immediately. Wouldn't have been so creeped out by him." Tanner couldn't tear his eyes away from all the pictures of Bree. Pictures of her with people. Without them. Some with the babies.

But no matter what the scene or the situation, she always had that stiff, pinched look on her face. In not one single picture was she smiling, even the ones with the babies.

She always looked scared.

He'd gotten so used to that look on her face that he didn't even notice it anymore.

Bree lived in terror.

He walked over to study one, obviously shot from a small camera at a low angle. Bree was standing with Mr. and Mrs. A, the babies and Judy. A couple of other people, features not seen in the shot, were loitering around, too. A crowd.

Despite all the people around her, Bree looked completely alone. A misfit among laughing, content people. Like she didn't know how to feel what they were feeling and didn't even want to try in case she failed.

Damn it. Tanner wanted to teach this woman how to smile. Wanted to provide her a safe place where she could learn to find the smile he knew was inside her.

Ronnie cleared his throat. "This guy is a psycho. Maybe we shouldn't have sent Bree off on her own if he's now following her."

"Wasn't she afraid she was going to end up in his basement? I thought she was being melodramatic when she said it yesterday, but now…" Scott held his hand out toward the pictures. "Maybe not. Are you sure we have no way of getting in touch with her? No phone number?"

Tanner shook his head. He wanted to tell Ronnie and Scott what was going on but couldn't. "Her phone was last seen in multiple pieces in her apartment. And she didn't give any forwarding address. So, as far as we're concerned, she's gone."

Ronnie and Scott were both staring at him like he'd just kicked a puppy into oncoming traffic. He couldn't blame them; just the thought of Bree being out there alone with someone this crazy after her made him sick.

"Look," he continued, "the best thing we can do for Bree is get an APB out for Steele and make sure all our contacts in other counties know he could be dangerous. Bree wanted out of this town. She's an adult, hasn't broken the law and we couldn't keep her here against her will. Maybe she was going to family or something."

"What do we know about Steele?" Scott asked. "Any record?"

Tanner shook his head. "Completely clean. After seeing this, I'm thinking probably a fake ID. Hopefully, the crime lab can get some prints and we can run them."

Scott looked around at the pictures again. "I just hope law enforcement finds him before he finds Bree. Because this is a man obsessed. And obsession is dangerous."

It was nearly four in the morning before Tanner made it back out to the ranch.

Processing Steele's apartment had taken hours, and Tanner had stayed to make sure the crime lab didn't miss anything. He didn't normally micromanage the department like this, but when it came to Steele, he couldn't afford any more slipups.

When the head lab technician told Tanner that they didn't get a single fingerprint from the entire place, he was angry but not surprised. Steele had wiped the place down before he left.

Back at the office, Scott had assisted in digging further into Bill Steele's identity. It hadn't taken long to discover the ID was fake.

Again, angry but not surprised.

When they'd gotten a call of a possible sighting of Steele in Jackson County, again in the direction Gavin had taken Bree's car, Tanner had driven there himself. If they caught Steele, he wanted to be the first to question him, before any other county decided they had dibs if his real identity came back as someone more dangerous.

But it had been a false alarm, costing Tanner three hours of his time. Time he couldn't afford when there was both a psycho and some sinister technology organization out to harm the woman he couldn't get off his mind.

He shouldn't have come at all, should've just stayed at his place in town. But despite trusting his brother implicitly, he needed to see with his own eyes that Bree was okay.

He rubbed the back of his neck as he got to the door, then held his hand up in a wave to Noah. He didn't bother looking around. He didn't know where his brother was, but Tanner had no doubt he was close.

Tanner let himself in the house, closing the door behind him, and just listened. Quiet.

But not the utter stillness that normally permeated his house when he arrived. There were signs of life everywhere. A bib resting on the kitchen table. One of the car seat carriers sitting on his couch. Bree's sweater hanging off the back of a chair.

He'd always purposely lived a solitary life. He'd known since he was ten he wanted to go into law enforcement, then had seen what it had done to his mother when his father died in the line of duty. And even before that, the long, odd hours—sometimes being called away in the middle of the night—and the general stress of this job had often placed a heavier burden on his parents' marriage.

So Tanner had always kept his relationships casual and simple, never planning to drag a woman into this life with him.

But nothing about Bree was casual.

And very definitely not simple.

He took off his holster and out of habit—niece and nephews—set it in the small gun safe next to the door. He kicked off his shoes and planned to grab a blanket out of the linen closet and immediately lie down on the couch.

He found himself walking into his bedroom instead.

Found himself stopping and staring at Bree lying curled in his king-size bed.

Found his breath stolen at the way moonlight shined through the window, casting an otherworldly glow on her long brown hair and delicate features.

At least in sleep she didn't have the same pinched and uncomfortable expression she'd had in all the photos he'd studied of her today. Like she would never know what it meant to fit in with other people.

Like she would always be alone.

He wanted to go to her and pull her up against him, tell her she didn't have to look like that anymore.

He took a step closer before he could stop himself then breathed out a curse as her eyes fluttered open, afraid he'd frightened her.

"Tanner?"

"Yeah, it's just me. Go back to sleep. I didn't mean to wake you up."

"Are you okay?" She reached out toward him, her voice soft, husky.

Sexy.

He took a rapid step backward.

Immediately a shuttered look fell over her features, slamming away the welcoming look that had resided there a moment before. "I'm sorry. Do you want your bed? I can get up."

He recognized her tight expression right away. God knew he'd seen it enough times in the pictures today. Uncertainty. Discomfort.

Isolation.

And he'd been the one to put that look in her eyes this time.

She withdrew the arm she'd reached out to him.

No, damn it. He wasn't going to let her withdraw from him.

He crossed until he was standing right next to her. "Actually, I would like my bed."

"Oh." She sat up. "Okay. Just let me—"

"No. I want it with you in it." Before either one of them overthought it, he reached down, took her slight weight in his arms and slid her over. Then got into the bed next to her.

He turned over onto his side then looped an arm around her waist and pulled her up against him.

For the first time since he'd gotten that message from Steele that Bree was in trouble, Tanner relaxed. She was in his house, his bed, his care.

He kissed her hair. “Go back to sleep. I just want to be with you. Even if it’s just for tonight.”

She didn’t say anything but a few moments later began to relax against him.

And everything about it felt right.

Chapter Twenty-One

When Bree woke up a few hours later, Tanner was gone. She saw so little of him for the next three days, she was almost convinced she'd imagined the whole thing.

Imagined lying in bed with his strong arms securely around her. Imagined feeling safe and secure and cherished for the first time in her life.

She knew why Tanner hadn't been around much. He'd explained about creepy, thin guy—Steele, or whatever his real name was—and his obsession with her and the twins. Tanner and Scott had been working around the clock trying to find him.

Bree couldn't even wrap her head around it. Only she could somehow gain a psycho stalker at the same time as being hunted by a deadly organization intent on her capture or death.

She knew Tanner had questions about the Organization. That it wouldn't be long until he began to press her for info.

Rightfully so.

Because what about Melissa? Except for that panicked conversation a few nights ago, Bree hadn't heard anything from her cousin in two weeks. Had no way to hear from her.

Had she been caught when she warned Bree?

Was she even still alive?

Bree refused to accept that her cousin was dead. But she also couldn't run from the truth any longer.

Melissa couldn't defeat the Organization. It didn't matter how motivated or determined she was. She just didn't have the hacking skills to get around their system.

Michael Jeter was a computer genius. He would have backup systems and trapdoors that someone like Melissa—even as competent as she was—wouldn't be able to get around.

He was the type of computer genius no one could beat.

Except another computer genius.

Here Bree sat on the steps of a ranch in the middle of Colorado, rising sun kissing her skin, healthy babies sleeping inside a warm, sturdy house.

Hell, she even had a pregnant dog sitting beside her supplying companionship, her master out somewhere providing protection against any threat that might come her way.

Bree was living a stolen life.

She was in someone else's house, with someone else's kids, even someone else's damn dog.

Even worse, she was stealing from people she *cared* about. And she had the means to stop it all if she wasn't a coward.

Melissa couldn't stop Michael Jeter.

But Bree could.

She lifted her face to the low-lying sun, breathing in

the air pungent with life. These porch steps, in less than a week, had made her feel more like she had a home—a place in the world—than her apartment in Kansas City ever had. And definitely more than any place she'd shared with her mom for a few months at a time.

But it wasn't her place. And it never would be—she would never be able to live with herself—if she didn't do what she could to help Melissa.

To ensure Christian and Beth had their mother around to raise them.

She heard Tanner pulling up long before his car parked in front of the house. He'd worked all night again to protect her, or hopefully caught a few hours' sleep at his place in town.

As Tanner's SUV door shut, a sharp whistle came from the trees on the other side of the property near the back of the house, and Corfu got up and trotted off.

"I guess Noah's babysitting duties are over for the day since you're home."

Tanner sat beside her. He was wearing his civilian clothes, including that cowboy hat that set her heart beating faster than it should. He didn't look too tired.

"He doesn't mind." He knocked her knee with his. "You okay?"

"No, I don't think so."

His browed furrowed together. "What happened?"

She wrapped both arms around her knees and pulled them to her chest. "I tried to pick up both Christian and Beth yesterday evening at the same time. They lunged for each other, and I nearly dropped them both."

He muttered a curse. "Did one of them get hurt?

Hell, did *you* get hurt? Those kids weigh a ton now. And they're more active than ever."

She leaned her head on her arms and studied him. "No, I got them under control and put one of them down. But you've just made my point. They're so big. They're growing more every day."

"Um, I think babies are supposed to do that."

She looked out at the horses again. "But they're not *my* babies. Every day that I get to hold them and feed them and play with them is another their mother misses out on."

"But I thought Melissa wanted you to keep them safe while she did whatever is needed to take down these people she works for."

Bree shook her head, hugging her legs tighter. It was time for complete honesty with Tanner.

Way past time.

"Melissa can't do it. Whatever she's doing is not going to be enough to stop them."

"How do you know?"

"Because I know who she's up against. I was part of that group before my mom got me away from them when I was thirteen."

"The Organization? That same group that you said was dangerous and would kill us all?"

She nodded.

Tanner ran a hand over his face. "I need you to tell me exactly what is going on. Exactly how you're involved and exactly what needs to be done to keep you and the kids safe."

"It's not an easy story to believe."

"Try me. *Trust me.*"

She stared out into the gathering dawn. "I never went to college. Never really went to school at all actually, after I turned thirteen. That's not to say I never had an education, just that I never went to the buildings like most other people did."

"You were homeschooled?"

"Sort of. More like, I was a genius-level hacker who could read three times as fast as most people and could visualize code twice as fast as that. So I taught myself everything I needed to know."

He nodded slowly, so she continued.

"My father died when I was just a baby, and my mom struggled to provide for us on a waitress's salary. I wasn't an easy kid. If you think I'm awkward and prickly now, you should've seen me then. When I was six, she realized I had a gift for computers."

More than a gift. So much more than a gift. A huge blessing.

And a curse.

"By the time I was eight, everyone in the entire school system for the whole county had taught me everything they knew. By that point, I was teaching them new things about coding and software development."

"You were a child prodigy. Like kids with the instruments."

"I guess, except a computer was my instrument rather than a violin or piano. But yes, I could—*can*—play it beautifully. That's how I came to the attention of Communication for All. You've heard of them?"

He took a sip of his coffee. "The charity group? Sure."

"They have schools for underprivileged children to

help them learn computer skills and hopefully better their lives."

"Sounds like a perfect fit for you."

She shook her head, remembering quite clearly how excited she'd been at eight and a half to finally be around people who understood her. Who knew as much about computers as she did and didn't think she was odd.

The people at Communication for All, especially Michael Jeter, revered her.

At least at first.

"I quickly got the attention of people high up in that organization. They wanted to groom me for important things. They brought me to live at one of their schools. My mom didn't want me there by myself, so they brought her, too. All expenses paid—my mom didn't have to pay for a thing and was even able to quit her job. They even brought my cousin, Melissa, since she also had skills beyond her years."

"Sounds like an amazing opportunity. I've always heard wonderful things about Communication for All."

Bree stared straight ahead. "No doubt you have." Everybody had.

"Yeah, I mean Michael Jeter has pretty much been termed an altruistic genius by every person who's ever..." Tanner faded out. *"Jeter."*

He stood with controlled movements. She wasn't surprised he was figuring it out. Tanner was too smart, too observant, not to piece it all together.

"That guy in the alley in Denver was talking to a Mr. Jeter." Tanner turned to her. "You stiffened at the name, but I misread your body language at the time. I thought it was because of the guys with the guns. But it was because Jeter was threatening to come there personally."

"When I was eleven, I outgrew most of the instructors at Communication for All. I knew more about system development and coding than they did. I was twelve when I backdoored into their main system and..."

Her whole life had changed that day. What had started out as preteen mischief and an attempt to show off had ended in a nightmare.

One she was still trying to wake up from.

"Bree?" Tanner sat back down beside her and wrapped an arm around her, pulling her against his chest.

God, he felt so strong. Like nothing could get through him. Nothing could break him.

But everyone could be broken. A twelve-year-old Bethany had learned that very quickly.

"I found out every dirty secret the inner board of Communication for All had. They're evil, Tanner. Human trafficking, weapons and information sales. They use their humanitarian front to get into places without much scrutiny."

He stiffened. She could almost hear his mind working, attempting to process it all. He stood up and began pacing again. "Good God."

"I know," she whispered. It was difficult to take it all in.

"Everybody can't be in on it," he finally said. "Communication for All must have a thousand employees. They couldn't keep it under wraps."

She shook her head, rubbing at the tension forming at the back of her neck. "Most of them don't know what's really going on. They are trying to achieve the admirable mission associated with Communication for All. It's a very select few, an inner core of about twenty-five people, who know the truth and are behind it all."

"And you discovered this was going on when you were twelve?"

"Yes," she whispered. "At that point they were just starting to dip their toes into utilizing cell phones for illegal data mining. Run-of-the-mill stuff at first... software that caused phones to report credit cards or bank account numbers to them. Then they expanded."

"Expanded how?"

"I didn't make up that stuff I told you in Denver. They're utilizing cell audio and video mechanisms to record data, even when cameras and microphones aren't actively running. I know you don't have a smartphone, but have you ever heard people complain about how fast the batteries run down even when they're not using them?"

He began pacing again. "Sure. All the time."

"That's the Communication for All system pulling data off their phone. Every time there's a system update, they use it to piggyback onto more phones."

He stopped and stared at her. "How many do they have now?"

"According to Melissa? Millions. And they can use those phones to record data anytime they want. To find anyone they want. It's basically making a worldwide information grid that they control. Nobody will be able to hide. And it's about to get so much larger."

"How?"

She rubbed her eyes with her fingers. "Three days from now is the International Technology Symposium in Denver. Major phone manufacturers will all be there. Communication for All will provide them with some wonderful bit of technology that will be a breakthrough of epic proportion. They'll be hailed as heroes when they offer it to manufacturers for free."

"But there's a catch."

She nodded. "The tiniest of Trojan horses. A few lines of code that would probably be missed, even if the manufacturers were suspicious and went over the coding line by line. But from such a trusted source like Communication for All that has no ulterior motive? No one will ever even suspect it."

He crossed his arms over his chest. "How do you know about it if you've been gone for ten years?"

She forced an even breath. "That Trojan horse was the last thing they tried to get me to build before my mom took me and ran. But I didn't do it. I could've, but I didn't. And it's taken them ten years to get caught back up."

"I'm surprised they didn't force you. You were only a kid. With everything they're capable of, I would think brutalizing a single child wouldn't have been out of their wheelhouse."

Even now, ten years later, bile pooled in her stomach as she thought about it. The memory of the sound of her own bones breaking a split second before the pain ripped through. Her body still woke her up in a cold sweat sometimes.

She forced the memory from her mind now as she wrapped her arms around her knees once again and pulled them against her chest.

She closed her eyes. "It wasn't beyond their capacity. They used starvation and sleep deprivation first, but then realized that wasn't conducive to me actually being able to get the Trojan horse made. So then they went with physical pain—broke my legs in three different places over the course of the year. Finally, they started torturing my mother to get me to cooperate. That worked best."

"God, Bree..."

"Bethany. Bethany Malone. That's my real name." And she hadn't been able to say it out loud in ten years. "Melissa named Beth after me. But I'm Bree now. Bethany Malone died ten years ago when she hobbled out of the Communication for All campus with a mother who was hanging on to the last grips of sanity."

Chapter Twenty-Two

Tanner wanted to grab Bree and pull her into his arms. To comfort both her and the child inside her who had suffered so much.

But the way she said it all with almost no emotion—how they tortured her and her mother—told him she wouldn't respond to comfort right now.

"My mom gave me eight hours and forty-five minutes' warning that she'd found a way to get out," Bree continued, her voice getting more and more distant. "I used that time to do as much damage to the Organization as I could. I made sure to set them back for years, while also erasing every image that had ever been taken of me or my mom. I didn't want them to be able to find us."

"That was smart of you."

"The damage I did to them in eight hours set them back *years*. I know for a fact Michael Jeter hated me after that. I wish I could've seen his face when he'd found out what I'd done."

But her own face got sadder, not happier. Tanner couldn't stay away anymore. He sat down and pulled her up against his chest. "You got out. You survived. You bested them. That's what matters."

"If I had worked that hard when they wanted me to, they wouldn't have hurt my mom. She never recovered, Tanner." She shook her head against his chest. "She never stopped looking over her shoulder, convinced the Organization was there. Never stopped being terrified. Even at the end, she was convinced she was being betrayed and the Organization was coming to get her."

Bree rubbed her shoulder in the peculiar way he'd seen her do multiple times in the last few weeks.

"She never got over it?"

"No. We moved around all the time. Sometimes we even lived apart if she thought they might be gaining on us. Split up a lot."

Which explained why she'd wanted to do that when they were in trouble.

"Toward the end..." She trailed off, rubbing the front of her shoulder again so hard he was afraid she was going to leave a mark on her skin.

He pressed his hand over hers so it lay flat against her shirt rather than moving. "Toward the end...she hurt you?"

Bree's eyes flew to his. "She didn't mean to. She was confused. Sick. The last few weeks, she was convinced I was working for the Organization. That I was helping them take us back into captivity."

That didn't make any sense, of course, but he didn't need to point that out. Bree was well aware her mother's fears had been irrational.

"She stabbed me in the shoulder because she thought I had poisoned her. Then she ran outside and right in front of a car. Killed her instantly."

He gripped her hand in his and brought it down from a wound that was years old but obviously had never healed. Might never heal.

He brought her fingers to his lips. “She needed more help than you could give her. She had a breakdown.”

“She needed a daughter who hadn’t let her mother be tortured until she was never right in the mind again!”

It was the most emotion he’d ever heard out of Bree.

He pulled her against his chest and wrapped his arms around her. “No. She sacrificed to get you out of there. She wouldn’t have wanted you to give the Organization what they were demanding. But her head muddied it up.”

She held herself stiff for a moment before relaxing against him with a sigh. “I know. I know she wanted us out of there. I just wish we could’ve gotten out earlier. That I had been smart enough to figure out how to do *that* rather than just useless computer stuff.”

“Useless? You formulated technology that was years before your time. And you were a child when you did it.”

“And then I destroyed most of it before I left.”

They sat in silence for a few minutes. Tanner wasn’t sure if that had been the right call or not. But it had definitely been the only choice a teenager who’d been tortured physically, mentally and emotionally had.

“Where does Melissa fit into this?”

“Melissa didn’t know what the Organization really was until recently. She lost everything.” Tanner listened as Bree told him about how Melissa’s fiancé had been killed and how she hid the babies so she could try to make her move against Communication for All.

“But she can’t do it,” Bree said. “She’s not good

enough. I've known that the whole time but ignored it because I've been afraid. They have to be stopped right now, and I'm the only one who can do it."

"That means coming out of hiding. I can put you in protective custody."

"No. I've been thinking about this all day. In order for this to work, I'll have to be at the symposium myself. I'll use their own system against them."

"I'll make sure you're safe." And he damn well meant it.

A soft sound came from the monitor. Beth was awake. She generally woke up from sleep first and played contentedly for a few minutes until Christian woke and made the entire world aware of his unhappiness.

Bree stood and pointed at the baby monitor. "Those kids need to grow up with their mom. Not with their emotionally stunted second cousin," she said.

Tanner stood also. "Technically, it's first cousin once removed."

Bree laughed, a beautiful sound he wanted to hear more of. "I notice you don't try to argue the *emotionally stunted* part."

He stepped closer. "You're emotionally *guarded*, not stunted. And that's completely understandable." He slid a hand under the thick brown hair at her nape. "There's absolutely nothing wrong with taking it slow. Believe me, slow can be very, very good."

He kissed her. Tenderly, aware that this woman—brilliant, brave and about to bring down a major group of criminals—had never known tender kisses. Outside of him, had probably never known any kisses at all.

He would be more than glad to show her any type of kiss she wanted to learn.

She sighed, leaning into him, her trim body brushing against his. He had to struggle to remember to remain tender and gentle.

When Bree's little tongue brushed against his lips, all thoughts of tender fled. His hands came up to cup her face, tilting her head so he had better access to those sweet lips.

He nibbled at them until they opened then deepened the kiss until it was a melding of their mouths, no space left between them. He knew he should slow things down, but Bree's arms wrapped snugly around the back of his neck weren't going to allow it anyway.

Not that he wanted to.

But still he was impossibly cognizant of the need to take this at a speed she could handle and process. No matter how much her lips were driving him crazy.

In the end it wasn't either of them who broke the kiss, it was Christian letting the world know he was awake.

Bree let out a sigh as they broke away from each other, but at least her eyes still met his. "That kid sure can scream," she whispered.

"If it wasn't for him crying, I never would've walked down that aisle at the drugstore. But I'm glad both of them aren't like that."

She let out a sigh and tilted her head against his chest. He would've gladly stood there forever and let her lean against him. "I don't have much time to stop the Organization. I have to start right away."

"What do you need?" he said against her hair.

"A safe place to work, preferably on a government

computer so I can more easily cover my tracks." She pulled back and looked up at him. "And someone to watch the twins. It's going to take every spare minute before the symposium for me to get inside the Organization's system. I won't be able to care for the babies the way they need. It nearly killed me when I was trying to do that before using the library's internet."

"That's why you were there in the middle of the night when you were supposed to be resting?" That made so much sense now.

Those green eyes widened. "How did you know?"

"I saw you there that night. I had no idea what you were doing."

She nodded. "I was trying to help Melissa. But she told me to stop and focus on the kids and let her worry about the Organization. I don't even know if she's still alive, Tanner. She might have risked it all calling me and telling me to get out of the apartment."

"I know people in federal law enforcement. Omega Sector can have someone knocking on Communication for All's door today. If she's still alive, we can get her out."

Bree thought about that for a moment. "No. If they didn't catch her, going in there will tip them off and we'll never be able to stop them. Mellie wants to be free. Wants the twins to be free. The only way that will happen is for me to stop them from the inside."

"Then we'll make it happen. Whatever you need. I'll make sure you have it. You're not alone in this anymore, Bree."

Her big green eyes blinked up at him. "I…I…" She faded off with a shrug.

He put a finger over her lips. "You don't have to know what to say. You don't even need to know what to feel right now. Let's go get those babies fed and then let you go to work so you can save the world."

Chapter Twenty-Three

After helping her feed the kids, Tanner left, telling Bree to pack up everything for the babies. She was crying by the time she got the second armful of baby stuff into the car Noah brought over.

She knew there was every possibility she might not see them again. Despite Tanner's assurances that they could handle the Organization, he and his federal law enforcement friends in Omega Sector who were waiting on standby really didn't have any idea of who they were up against.

Tanner thought he could protect her, but she still knew the odds were that she would be dead or, worse, back in the Organization's clutches by the time the symposium was done.

She couldn't live through that again.

But she couldn't do nothing any longer, either.

"You want help loading?" Noah asked. He was standing at the end of the porch, Corfu at his feet.

"No. It's not heavy. I'm just an emotional basket case."

Noah didn't try to argue or placate her. She appreciated that. “Being close to people is hard,” he said. “The price is high.”

“Too high?” she muttered, more to herself than him.

He answered anyway. “Almost always.”

Right at this moment, she didn’t disagree with him. How much simpler her life would’ve been if she’d never opened the door to Melissa in the first place.

She placed the last load of stuff in the car. But how much emptier.

Would it be worth it in the end?

She knew when Tanner was about to show back up by the way Noah disappeared without a word. Sure enough, a car pulled up the long driveway a few moments later.

But when she saw who it was with Tanner, Bree almost burst into tears again.

Dan and Cheryl.

When they rushed out of the car and hugged her, this time, for the first time, she hugged them back.

“Oh, sweetheart! You’re okay!” Cheryl kept her arms around Bree almost in a choke hold, but Bree didn’t mind. “When Tanner told us what was going on, we came right over here to help. I’m so glad you’re safe.”

“And I’m so glad I will eventually heal from the bruises Mrs. A’s smacks gave me when she found out you were here and that I hadn’t really run you out of town,” Tanner muttered.

But he grinned and winked at Bree from where she remained trapped in Cheryl’s arms.

“Dan and Cheryl are going to take the twins and leave town,” Tanner explained.

Cheryl finally pulled back. “We’re going to go visit

my son and his wife in Texas. Stay completely out of the fray. Tanner explained that you're doing something important and dangerous."

"Yes."

Dan placed himself so he was between her and Tanner. "Bree, you don't have to. You can come with us and the babies. We'll hide out until this all blows over."

She reached out and grabbed Dan's hand, something she wouldn't have been able to do a month ago. "This will never blow over. I have to make a stand here or the babies and I will never be safe."

Once the Organization uploaded the software to the phones, they would be able to find her no matter where she hid.

"Okay," Dan said. "I just wanted you to know you have a choice."

She squeezed his hand. "This is my choice."

"And I'm going to make sure she's safe," Tanner said. "If they want to get to her, they're going to have to go through me."

They all spent the next few minutes getting the babies ready for their road trip. Bree kissed them both tenderly before placing them into the car seats. Way before she was ready, they were pulling away.

Bree didn't cry. Didn't stare after the car. Didn't let herself dwell on the fact that she might never see Christian and Beth again.

Instead she pulled on every bit of strength she'd developed from years of living on her own—strength her mother had instilled in Bree before her own strength disappeared—and turned to Tanner.

"It's time to get to work."

The Organization had stolen way too much of her life. She wasn't going to let them steal any more.

TANNER HAD NEVER seen someone do what Bree could do with a computer. She had been working for nearly three days straight to try to get into Communication for All's inner computer system.

She'd tried to explain exactly what she was doing the first day, but he hadn't understood ninety percent of what she said. So he'd just tugged on her ponytail until she'd looked up from the computer screen and kissed her to shut her up.

He was pretty sure her fingers hadn't stopped typing the whole time.

The woman was completely focused on the task at hand.

He'd been tempted to distract her. To force her out of the emotionless bubble she'd encased herself in, because the bubble hadn't included him.

Any other time he would. He had no plans to let Bree shut him out just because she'd always kept people shut out in the past.

But right now that bubble was what was allowing her to function. To stay firmly committed to the task at hand and take down these murderous bastards.

They'd set up Bree's workspace in the Sunrise, since it was closed while the Andrewses were gone. She was working in the office, a space already familiar to her, which gave her access to food and a bathroom, and didn't have any windows that would allow someone to spot her.

Plus, the Andrewses' absence gave Tanner the excuse to look in on the diner without suspicion. Noah and some more of his former Special Forces friends from Wyoming were providing invisible around-the-clock security for Bree, since Tanner couldn't do it.

Tanner was being watched. He had no doubt about it. The question was, by who?

Had Steele backtracked to Risk Peak, looking for Bree? Had the Organization sent someone else to see if they could find her here?

Or maybe it was just the townspeople who were still angry with him for sending Bree off on her own, and then, worse, causing the town's favorite diner to shut down for a couple weeks because the Andrewses were so heartbroken.

Tanner could take the evil eye from the town. But he knew they were running out of time. The symposium was in just a few hours, and Bree was exhausted. She hadn't gotten more than a couple hours' sleep here and there since she started. Hadn't even stopped for a full meal.

Tanner didn't like it. Every instinct had him wanting to pamper and protect her, and teach her how to accept it.

And he would. But right now he would accept/acknowledge she was a woman on a mission and he was backup. So he would encourage her strength.

He let himself in the back door of the Sunrise like he had each day. He walked over and kissed Bree on the top of the head before removing the plates and cups piled up by the Grand County laptop she was using.

"We've got a problem," she said. Her fingers stopped typing.

That wasn't a good sign.

"How bad?"

"The Organization knows I'm in Risk Peak. They don't know who I am or what exactly I'm doing, but they know someone's pushing at them."

He muttered a curse. "We've got to get you out of here."

"I can't leave now. I'm too close to breaking through, and we're out of time. We need to leave for the symposium in no more than six hours in order for this to work." She looked up at him with those green eyes. "Tanner, I need you to buy me some time. Make them think I'm somewhere else. But they're going to be monitoring every cellular transmission anywhere they can within a fifty-mile radius of here."

Tanner pulled out his dumb phone. "This still safe?"

She nodded. "Until tomorrow. Once the Organization's new system goes live and they start piggybacking off the manufacturers' systems, then no cellular phone will be safe. Every phone will broadcast data to the Organization. But I still wouldn't use it just in case I'm wrong."

"You keep working. I'll buy you the time you need."

She gave him a tired smile before her eyes and hands were back on the laptop in front of her.

Tanner turned on the back light of the diner, his signal to Noah that they needed to meet. A few minutes later, Noah showed up. Tanner led him into the kitchen so they could talk without disturbing Bree.

"Bree says the Organization is onto her. We need to set up a decoy, get her the space and time she needs. And we should deem all cell phones no longer safe."

Noah grunted. "We can set something up at the ranch. Make them think she's there. It would give you and me the tactical advantage since we know it so well. And my team is fully capable."

Tanner had made the decision not to bring in law enforcement. Official channels meant too many modes of communication that could be monitored.

"Yeah, good. I've got my federal colleagues in Denver as soon as Bree cracks the system and we've got the proof we need that Communication for All is dirty."

Noah nodded. "One way or another, it ends today. How are we going to get our bad guys out to the ranch?"

"They don't know we're onto them," Tanner said. "So we use cell phones against them."

Noah smiled. "And then we take them out of commission. My kind of plan."

"I'm going to have to bring Ronnie in on it. I'll leave him here as guard for Bree. She's not going to notice if either of us are missing anyway. A bomb could go off and I'm not sure she would notice."

"I'll get my team out to the ranch and will be waiting for your call."

A moment later, Noah was gone.

Tanner walked back into the office and crouched down beside Bree. She stopped what she was doing and looked at him.

"We're leading them away," he said. "You keep

working. I'll send Ronnie to guard but will tell him not to disturb you."

Her lips pursed. "I know I can do it, but I don't know if I can do it in *time*."

He reached over and kissed her softly. "You can."

This time when his lips met hers, she clung to him. He groaned against her mouth. "There's nothing I want to do more than stay here and kiss you, but we've both got to get to work."

"Be careful." She clutched him closer to her for just a second. "The Organization is dangerous and smart."

He smiled. "So are we. We'll buy you the time you need."

She straightened. "I won't waste it."

He pulled her in for a tight embrace and kissed the top of her head. "I know."

Her fingers were already flying on the keyboard as he walked briskly out the door.

Back at the station a few minutes later, he found Ronnie at his desk.

"Ronnie, can I see you for a second in my office?"

The deputy nodded and followed him in.

"I don't have any further updates about Steele, if that's what—"

Tanner cut him off. "I need to borrow your personal phone to make a call."

Ronnie eyed both the phone sitting on Tanner's desk and the one clipped at his waist. Probably just being in the same room with Ronnie's smartphone meant the Organization was listening, but Tanner wanted to make sure they got this message loud and clear.

"Um, sure."

"You'll understand in a minute."

Ronnie entered his password and handed the phone to Tanner. Tanner immediately punched in his brother's number.

"Dempsey."

Noah's greeting was terse. If it hadn't been for this situation, he probably wouldn't have answered at all.

"Noah, it's Tanner. I'm using Ronnie's phone because I think mine might be bugged."

Right on cue, Noah muttered a curse.

"Is Bree okay?" Tanner asked.

"Yeah. I've got to admit I never expected to see her face here again. She's looking pretty tired and hasn't gotten up from her computer since she arrived."

Good job. Give them something to make them nervous.

"I can't get home until this evening. Too many people around, and I feel like I'm being watched."

"That's fine. Like I said, she's busy with her computer stuff here in your kitchen. She's excited. Talking about bringing down some sort of organization."

Tanner winced. They were trying to buy time, not cause the Organization to bomb the ranch.

Noah was spoiling for a fight. Wanted them to send out the troops.

That was fine, because so was Tanner.

"Just keep her in my house until I can get home. Make sure she doesn't run off again."

"Will do, bro. Since nobody knows she's here, I'll just be back and forth between my place and yours."

"Okay," Tanner said. "Just keep an eye out. I don't want her running off again until we get some answers."

"Roger that." Noah disconnected the call.

Tanner looked at Ronnie but didn't hand him back his phone.

"Holy hell, boss. What exactly is going on?"

"Let's go out back and have a cigarette."

Before Ronnie could respond that neither of them smoked, Tanner held a finger up to his lips in a gesture for quiet.

He threw the other man's phone in a drawer and led him outside.

Ronnie looked all sorts of confused. "Do you really think your phone is bugged?"

"I think it's way more than that. And I'm going to need your help."

"Providing backup at your ranch? Do you think Steele might make an attempt for Bree?"

"We've got much bigger problems than Bill Steele, or whatever his name is. And Bree is not at my ranch."

"But you and Noah just said—"

"I said that specifically for the ears that were listening. And those ears are listening to *any* cell phone, off or on. I don't have time to go into the details right now. You're just going to have to trust me."

Ronnie nodded. "What do you need me to do?"

Tanner was thankful he and Ronnie had been working together for so long. "Bree is at the Sunrise. I need you to watch over her while Noah and I do some hunting."

"Sure, I—"

They broke off from the conversation as Scott walked outside and saw them.

"You letting him in on it?" Ronnie muttered softly.

Tanner gave a short shake of his head. It wasn't that he didn't trust the kid; as a matter of fact, Scott had been almost more ferocious in the search for Steele than anyone. But Scott was leaving soon, and Tanner didn't want to put him in any unnecessary danger.

Scott gave them a friendly smile as he joined them. "Hey, somebody told me you were out here. I'm just about done with everything and will be heading out this afternoon. I'm just missing one laptop to place the final training software on. It's an older one, and no one seems to quite know where to find it."

That would be because Bree was currently using it to try to work her magic. But Tanner didn't have time to come up with a reasonable lie. He needed to get to the ranch since the plan was already in motion.

"Honestly, I'm not sure where that thing is. I'll just install the update myself once it's located."

"Oh, okay." Scott shrugged and gave a half smile. "Well, then, I guess this is goodbye. I'm moving on to Colorado Springs today."

"Thanks for your help this past week. I know I wasn't the best of company, but I appreciate you trying to help us track down Steele. That went above and beyond what you were here to do."

Scott's chubby face broke into a smile. "It was no problem. Sorry I couldn't do more to find him. He's a slippery bastard."

Was he one of the people on their way to Tanner's ranch right now?

He reached out to shake Scott's hand. "I visit different departments quite a bit. I'll try to touch base with you and see if we can go have a beer sometime."

"I'd like that."

Tanner gave both men a brief nod then hustled toward his SUV.

It was time to catch some bad guys.

Chapter Twenty-Four

Tanner may have never fought side by side with his brother in battle, but there was damn well no one else he'd rather have at his back right now when it came to protecting Bree. Having three more of Noah's highly qualified former army team members here was just a bonus.

Tanner and Noah were currently standing in the tree line, just to the side of Tanner's house. Noah had binoculars and was scoping everything out around them. Every once in a while, he would use hand gestures to signal to his teammates. None of them were willing to take a chance communicating over phones or radios.

They would have to do things old-school.

Just over an hour after Tanner made the fake phone call to Noah, the action began.

"Looks like we've got four coming in on foot from the south. They're making a stealth approach directly toward the house," Noah said after looking through his binoculars. The two of them did not have that area in their sights; Noah was reporting back whatever his team was signaling to him.

The plan was to let them come. To let them get as

close as possible and think that Bree was here for as long as possible. Buy her as much time as they could.

"They're dressed in suits. Not ready for the terrain." Noah rolled his eyes. "This is almost too easy."

Tanner kept a close eye on the house. "Remember the plan. We string them along, take them down, but nobody gets killed. Make sure your people know that."

"They know. If that wasn't the case, there'd already be four suits on the ground."

A couple minutes later, they could hear an engine of a vehicle making an approach down their long driveway. Tanner brought his own binoculars up. "What a surprise. It looks like the power company has chosen today to pay a visit."

They both knew that was not the power company coming up their drive.

"We must've forgotten to pay the bill and they're coming to collect," Noah said dryly.

"Bet you five dollars they go with faulty wiring as their excuse. It looks like there's two guys in the front seat of the van. Possibly more in the back."

"The van is probably the signal for those guys in the woods to close in."

Tanner nodded. He agreed. That would be the smart play.

"Have your team take out the people coming in on foot. Make sure they aren't able to send out a signal or message. If someone gets word out, this is all for nothing."

"Roger that."

"Noah, remember, no body bags."

Noah just grinned. Tanner left him to signal the information to his team, watching the van get closer. It would be up to him and his brother to take down however many *power company* guys were coming their way.

Surprise was the best element they had. The Organization was only expecting Noah and Bree to be here, so they weren't expecting much resistance. They'd also be complacent, thinking backup in the woods was just moments away.

By the time Noah was finished communicating with his team, Tanner had a plan. "You go out there and talk to them since they're expecting you. You handle the two in the front seat, and I'll handle whatever's in the back."

"You sure? Could be a ton of trouble in the back. You're going in there blind."

"Or it could be a half dozen dancing monkeys. I can handle myself."

Noah slapped him on the shoulder. "I know it."

Noah stepping out of the shadows proved he meant it. There was no going back now. If everybody didn't hold up their end of the task—if any of these bad guys got a single call out—this was all for nothing.

As the van got closer, Tanner turned and made his way silently through the trees so that he would be able to approach from the back. He stepped closer as the vehicle pulled to a stop directly in front of Tanner's house.

Both men got out of the front in Colorado power company uniforms.

"Mr. Dempsey? We're with the power company. We've received an urgent report that the wiring in some of the houses in this area is faulty and extremely dangerous."

Ha, Noah, you owe me five dollars.

"Is that so?" Noah replied. "I've never had any problems. Not even so much as a single flicker."

Tanner made his way closer to the back of the van.

"It's good that you're not inside the house," the second man said. "We've had reports of unexpected fires. There have even been some severe injuries."

Tanner recognized that voice. It was the same one who'd called Mr. Jeter in Denver. If Tanner had had any doubt about this not being the real power company, it was completely gone now. Not that he'd had much doubt. In the twelve years he'd owned this house, the power had been out here a grand total of zero times.

Tanner took a few steps closer. It wouldn't be long before whoever was in the back came out to provide assistance.

Tanner wanted to be right at the door when they did.

"Is there anyone else inside the house, sir?" the first guy asked. "It's important they come out right now."

"Right now? It's really that dangerous?" Noah played his part well. "I have a friend doing some important work on a computer."

"Yes, sir," Denver guy said. "If you could just call your friend out right now. We can't let you go back inside. It's too dangerous."

Too dangerous for them to risk letting him out of their sights. Did they have orders to kill the would-be Bree immediately, or take her back into the Organization?

"Hey, Bree, can you come out here for a second? It's important," Noah called out.

The back van door creaked open. That must have been the cue they were waiting for. Tanner stepped to the side of the van. He and Noah would have to time this perfectly.

"Can you call her again, sir?"

"How about if I just go in there and get her. This is ridiculous. The house isn't going to blow up in the thirty seconds it takes me to get her."

"I'm sorry, we can't let you do that." Denver's voice was farther from the van, closer to Noah.

"Hey, man, get your hands off me. You don't have any right to tell me whether I can or cannot go into my own house."

There was a scuffle, and Tanner didn't wait any longer. Noah would take care of those guys. Tanner had his own bad guys to worry about. It ended up being three. Not dancing monkeys after all.

The first two were out of the vehicle and the third was on his way when Tanner rounded the back.

He immediately slammed the door against the head of the man climbing out, glancing over to make sure he was unconscious before facing the other two men.

Something jolted hard against the front of the van, and Tanner prayed it wasn't Noah.

Tanner didn't waste any time. He dived for the closest man, being sure to knock the phone out of the hand of the second guy. That bought Tanner a little time, but not much.

Fighting two men was never easy. Keeping them from using their weapons, phones or even calling out to whatever transmitting devices might pick up their voices was damned near impossible.

His flying punch connected with the first man's jaw, and he kicked out backward with his foot to land in that guy's stomach. Tanner grunted as he took a solid hook to the jaw from the first man, and saw the second man reaching for his gun from the corner of his eye. Tanner brought his elbow up and around into the face of the first man, hearing the unmistakable crack of a breaking nose.

As that guy howled, Tanner turned toward the second, diving for him to keep him from getting his weapon out. He knocked the gun from his hand and sent it skittering across the drive.

Tanner didn't hesitate. Three quick punches and the second guy was on the ground, unconscious. He jumped up, spun and a roundhouse kick to the first man had him lying next to his buddy.

The third guy, who was just starting to get his senses back after being knocked on the head by the door, groaned and began crawling toward the back of the van again.

Tanner just slammed the door against his head again, since it worked so well the first time, and watched him fall.

Noah came running around the van. "You clear?"

Tanner nodded, sucking in air to catch his breath, wincing at the blows he'd taken. Noah tossed him some zip ties and bandannas to use as gags, and soon all five men were restrained and sat up against the van. A few minutes later, the other four were dragged in by Noah's teammates, also tied and gagged.

Noah and Tanner walked so they could speak freely without the transmitters hearing them, while the rest of the team stood guard.

"It won't take the Organization long to figure out that

their team is out of commission," Noah said. "Then they're going to start the hunt for Bree all over. Wiser this time, because they know we're onto them."

Tanner wiped at a little bit of blood that had formed at the corner of his lip. "I know. But I'll be leaving with Bree for Denver in a couple of hours. Hopefully it will buy us that long. Once she's into their system and has the proof we need, Omega Sector can handle the arrests from there."

Noah nodded. "I hope it's enough."

Tanner did, too. "I've got to get out of here. If not, it will raise too many questions about why I didn't go through official channels."

"Okay, take off. I'll call this in, in a little while. State that I thought someone was trying to rob me. Maybe that will buy another hour or two."

Tanner clapped Noah on the shoulder. "Thank you—to you and your team—for what you did here today."

"Are you kidding? Taking down asshole bad guys is what we live for. No thanks needed. Just bring some that are a little tougher next time."

Tanner grinned and jogged toward his SUV. He wanted to check on Bree. They may have bought some time, but that didn't mean she was out of danger. And while he trusted Ronnie, he wanted her back in his sights.

Permanently.

And wasn't that scary as hell, considering he'd only kissed the woman a handful of times and she had more locks on her emotions than Fort Knox.

He planned to unlock every single one, picking a few if he needed to.

He made it back into Risk Peak in record time, parking his car at the station, intending to go straight to the Sunrise. But Gayle caught him in the parking lot. She was still mad at him for chasing Bree out of town. Before he could say anything, she held up a hand.

"I'm not going to ask you exactly what is going on. God knows I worked long enough for your father without always having the details. I trusted him, and I trust you."

Tanner let out a breath. "I promise I'll explain when I can."

"This has something to do with that girl, doesn't it?"

He nodded, glad she hadn't said Bree's name out loud.

"Fine," Gayle continued. "I'm glad to hear you're doing the right thing by her."

"That's my plan." He gave her a nod and turned toward the diner.

"Oh, and I gave Scott the location of the last laptop like you wanted."

Tanner stopped in his tracks. "What?"

She looked confused. "He said you said it was critical that he finish this last laptop before he left. So I looked it up on that system we installed a couple of years ago when we were doing the county-wide inventory."

Tanner blew out a harsh breath. "Scott? I told him I would do it."

"Well, that's not how he understood it. He was adamant that he get a hold of it immediately. It was over at the Sunrise for some reason, so—"

"When?" His heart began to slam against his chest.

"Maybe an hour ago? I'm not sure—"

Tanner didn't listen to the rest. He ran as fast as he could toward the diner.

The enemy had been hiding in plain sight all along.

Chapter Twenty-Five

Bree grinned at the screen in front of her.

She'd done it. She'd outmaneuvered the Organization.

Take that, you rat bastards.

They thought like criminals, and ultimately that had been their downfall, providing her the way into their system. Everything the Organization did was in shadows and back channels.

They weren't expecting someone to come straight up and knock on their figurative front door. There had just been the smallest crack of an opening, the tiniest of weaknesses, ones they wouldn't even have seen because they weren't her.

But that was all that Bree needed.

Her data was saved from the computer onto a SIM card. Now all she had to do was upload it to any member of the Organization's phone in the vicinity of the Denver symposium, and when the Organization tried to pull their little stunt where they took over all the cell phones in the world, they'd be in for quite a surprise.

Instead of being the ones controlling the information about everyone else, the entire world would have all the dirty laundry about *them.*

Every compromised member of Communication for All would be exposed. But hopefully the charity itself could live on.

Ronnie had been here with her in the office for a while, but his presence had been throwing her off, so he'd gone out into the main section of the diner. Whatever Tanner had done to gain her these last couple of hours, it had been worth it.

She sat back in her chair and grinned. They were going to take the Organization down. She never would've thought it was possible.

And couldn't even begin to think what her life might possibly be like after today. But making sure Melissa and the twins were safe was all that mattered.

"You know, when I met you, I knew you were more than a waitress, but I had no idea who you really were."

Bree turned with a gasp and found Scott standing in the door of the office.

Blood was dripping from a knife in his hand.

He held it up and inspected it. "I'm afraid Ronnie had an accident."

Bree spun around in the office that had provided her with a sense of security because it had no windows. But that also meant there were no other exits—something she hadn't even thought about until now. Her mother would've been so disappointed.

All it takes is one slipup and you're dead.

Looked like this was Bree's.

Scott took a step farther inside the room. "You

know the great thing about looking like a pudgy middle schooler? Nobody tends to think of you as a threat."

Bree took a step back as he took one forward. "You work for the Organization?"

He gave her a slimy smile, and she wondered how she'd ever thought of him as charming. Then winked at her. "I was handpicked for this mission by Mr. Jeter himself when we first realized someone on the inside was keeping tabs on someone in this town."

He shook his head in wonder. "Who would've thought that the greatest hacker who ever lived was not only alive, but had started the cutest little family of her own? Where are the screaming brats? I'm sure Mr. Jeter would like to meet them."

Just the sound of Jeter's name had nausea curdling her stomach. "They're not here. They're far away from here."

"Don't worry. We'll find them." Scott wiped off the handle of the knife with a napkin and grabbed her hand before she realized what he was going to do. He forced her fingers around the handle.

She let go as soon as he released her fingers, but it was too late. Her fingerprints were already on the weapon.

"You can consider that your going-away present to Tanner. A murder weapon with your prints on it seems like a pretty good reason for you to leave town without saying goodbye, don't you think?"

"R-Ronnie is dead?"

Scott shrugged. "Will be soon, if he's not dead yet. Too bad, really, I kind of liked him. But Mr. Jeter told me to bring you straight to him. It's a big day for Communication for All, you know. Mr. Jeter is going to be a hero."

She reached over and slid the SIM card into her hand before stuffing it into her pocket. Scott was about to hand deliver her where she needed to go anyway. Maybe she could upload the data before they killed her.

Although no one was likely to just lend her their phone.

Scott grabbed her hands and slid a zip tie around her wrists, pulling it tight, and began yanking her toward the back door.

"If you yell once we're outside, I'll kill whoever comes."

Bree believed him and kept her mouth shut.

She kept it shut on the ride to Denver, trying to come up with a plan. If she couldn't upload the data on the SIM card, no one would ever be able to gain proof about the Organization's illegal activities. They'd be untouchable.

And what about Tanner? Would he think she'd lied? Killed Ronnie?

The closer they got to Denver, the more fear seemed to swallow her whole. Panic crawled all over her body by the time Scott dragged her from an underground parking lot into a private suite that was part of the convention center.

He pushed her through the door and closed it behind him.

All she could see was Michael Jeter.

Terror slammed into her. She tried to remind herself that he was just a man, not a very big one at that. But all she could remember was the pain, the fear, the sound of her own bones breaking and her mother sobbing in pain as Jeter told her to focus. Concentrate. Do the work on the computer in front of her.

"Bethany!" Fingers snapped in front of her face, and she blinked back into the present. It was Jeter, of course. He'd never had any tolerance for people not doing exactly what he wanted at the moment he demanded it.

Who cared if they were terrified or traumatized or tortured?

Bree sucked in a deep breath, forcing oxygen into lungs that burned. She had to keep it together.

A sound caught her attention from the corner. Melissa sat on a couch crying softly. She'd obviously been beaten.

Bree's eyes flew back to Jeter as he spoke. "I'm so glad you're here, Bethany. I'm sure your cousin is, as well. We weren't sure if she knew where to find you or not."

"You bastard."

"I'm sure it must look that way to you. But you're not a child any longer. You can't use that as an excuse not to see the big picture."

She wanted to curse at him. To rage, strike him, hurt him the way he'd hurt her and the people she loved.

But there was only one way to take down the Organization today. And that was by being smart.

She held up her wrists in front of her face. "Your lackey bound my hands too tightly. Have someone cut me loose before I have permanent nerve damage. I won't be much good to you then."

Jeter's eyes narrowed. Obviously, he liked it better when she'd been cowering in fear a few moments ago.

Swallowing the terror that wasn't far from the surface, she raised an eyebrow.

Your move.

Jeter gestured with his head, and the guard came over and cut her hands loose. She rubbed at her aching wrists.

"I knew it was you, Bethany. Over the last couple of days when we first spotted someone trying to piggyback on our servers, I *knew* it was you. I've always known you would come back to me."

She glanced over at the clock. There were less than ten minutes before the cell phone update went live. She had to get the data on the SIM card uploaded to a phone by then.

She turned to Jeter. "You tortured me and my mother. Why would you think I would ever come back to you?"

Jeter continued as if she hadn't spoken. "And the fact that it's today, the day that history will revere me as a hero, makes it even more fitting. You were always supposed to be here when this happened. Be by my side. That would've happened years ago if you hadn't run."

He put his hands on his hips, moving his suit jacket to the side, and she saw what she needed. On one hip sat a smartphone clipped into his belt.

On the other was a holstered gun.

Either could work.

"I'm not excited that you went and had children, Bethany. That you let some other man touch you. But don't worry, we'll use them to keep you in line this time."

Melissa began crying harder.

Praying he wouldn't stop her, Bree walked toward

Melissa, sticking a hand in her pocket as she went, fishing out the tiny SIM card. She sat down by her cousin. "You're upsetting Melissa by talking about hurting innocent children, Michael."

His nostrils flared and his lips turned up a little. He liked her calling him Michael—the sense of intimacy it implied. Her stomach churned, but it was something she could use.

She covered Melissa's hands with hers. "It's okay," Bree crooned. "I'm not going to let anything happen. Crisscross, applesauce."

She pressed the SIM card into Melissa's palm as she said the words.

Melissa sniffled again, brows pulling together in confusion, but she didn't draw any attention to the SIM card.

"I'm glad you're here, Mellie. I don't think I could do this on my own. But don't cry anymore, okay?"

Melissa nodded. Bree stood and walked back toward Jeter, even though every instinct and memory told her to stay as far from him as possible.

"We could've done a lot together," she said.

He tilted his head to the side. "Oh, we still will. You're the only person who's ever come close to being my equal."

Scott snorted from the opposite side of the room, but they both ignored him. "You taught me a lot," she whispered.

Jeter's lips narrowed. "I taught you everything you know. I thought for a while that you were smarter than me, but the last few days have showed me otherwise. I was disappointed with how you came at our system, Bethany. Surely you must have realized that you couldn't shut us down remotely. What sort of genius would I be if I couldn't stop that sort of attack?"

The kind that was so conceited that a straightforward approach would slide right under his radar.

She took a step closer, and the guard cleared his throat. "Mr. Jeter…"

"She's fine," Jeter snapped, holding out a hand when the guard started to move toward them. Jeter himself closed the distance between them, reaching out to cup her cheek.

It was only by sheer strength of will that she kept herself from shuddering at his touch. She hoped Melissa was ready. They would only get one chance at this.

"You need guidance, Bethany. Discipline. You always have. I can be your greatest teacher. Together we can literally rule the world."

Even if she had had more time, she couldn't have stood one more second of hearing his voice, of feeling his hands on her.

She lunged for Jeter's waist. She knocked the cell phone off his belt and kicked it toward Melissa, praying she would understand what needed to be done.

Then Bree dived for the gun.

But Jeter had already recovered. His gun was out of his holster, in his hand and pointed at her face.

She took a step back.

"I can't tell you how disappointed I am that you did that, Bethany. And that you weren't smart enough to figure out what side of my waist the gun was on before making your move."

Melissa sobbed louder from behind her. Bree prayed it was to cover putting the SIM card into Jeter's phone.

Because they were out of time in more ways than one.

The gun remained pointed in her face. "Maybe you're not as smart as I think you are. Maybe like everyone else you're just a disappointment. Maybe I'd be better off getting rid of you right now."

"Maybe I never planned to remote hack you."

His eyes narrowed to slits. "What?"

"Mellie?"

"Done," her cousin responded.

"I'm still smarter than you, Jeter. I was when I was a kid and I am now."

For the first time, he looked worried. "Whatever you think you're going to do, you're too late. The update just went live."

Scott cursed from over in the corner. "Um, boss? We've got a problem."

Bree smiled as Scott continued to curse.

Jeter turned from her to glare at Scott. "What exactly is the problem?"

When Scott finally looked up from his phone, all color was gone from his normally ruddy cheeks. "Did you do this?"

Bree just continued to smile.

"We need to get out of here right now," Scott said. "She fooled us all. Instead of sending out our code, the update just sent out all the details about the Organization's illegal activities."

"To who?" Jeter sputtered.

"Everyone."

Bree glanced to the side as Melissa stood and held Jeter's phone out in front of her. "Looks like she's always going to be smarter than you, Jeter."

He pressed the gun against Bree's forehead. "Not if she's dead."

Chapter Twenty-Six

Scott had played them all from the beginning.

As soon as Ronnie had been taken by the ambulance, Tanner was in his vehicle, headed toward Denver. Every minute that passed seemed like an eternity.

No one from law enforcement—even the prestigious Omega Sector—could move in on Michael Jeter without a warrant. And no judge was willing to grant one on the day where Jeter was about to change the course of history by providing a huge technology breakthrough free to everyone.

And trying to explain that the huge technology breakthrough was actually part of a terrorist plot didn't go over well.

He'd called in a favor and had the lab immediately run the prints on the knife that had been used to stab Ronnie, hoping there might be a link to Jeter. But the prints had been Bree's. Or, more specifically, Bethany Malone's.

Tanner damned well knew Bree had not stabbed Ronnie. He didn't care what it looked like.

But he was on his own trying to find her. And his chances of being able to get to Jeter on this day—when he'd been the keynote speaker of a huge event a few hours ago—were slim to none.

He pulled up to the convention center downtown, parking illegally, flashing his badge at everyone until it got him to someone high enough to tell him where Michel Jeter was located.

"It's an emergency," he told a Mr. Kenyon, the manager of the building. "I need to see Jeter immediately."

Kenyon was maddeningly calm. "I have placed a call to Mr. Jeter's assistant with your request. I told him it was an emergency, but since you can't give me any other details about said emergency, I'm afraid no one seems to be taking your request seriously."

Kenyon gave Tanner a big, toothy smile. Tanner had to force himself not to punch him in it, or follow him when Kenyon turned and walked back into his office.

Tanner's fingers itched as they fell on the holster at his waist. If he pulled his weapon right now, he could get to Jeter. Get to Bree. Force Kenyon and his big smile to show him where they were.

It would be the end of his law enforcement career. But if it got Bree out of this alive, it would be worth it.

Saying a prayer, he flipped the snap off his holster.

"Save your theatrics, Dempsey," a voice said from behind him. "I can take you to Jeter without you doing time for terrorizing a building manager when this is said and done."

Tanner recognized that voice, and he had his weapon coming out of the holster anyway, spinning to face the man behind him.

Creepy, thin man. "Steele."

Steele held out his hands at shoulder height. "Actually, my name is Chris Martinez."

Tanner didn't lower his weapon. "Is that name supposed to mean something to me?"

"Perhaps if I say my full name is Christian, and that the love of my life named one of our children after me, it might ring a bell."

Now he lowered his weapon. "You're the twins' father?"

"Yes. And I worked for the Organization before they had me killed. Or almost had me killed. It's been a long recovery."

It explained some of the man's thinness. And so much else.

"I would love to answer all the three hundred questions burning in your eyes right now, but it will have to wait. I know where Jeter is."

"How?" Tanner asked.

"I'm not nearly as good as Bree with computers, but I know my way around one enough to be able to hack food services and find out where private meals are being delivered."

Tanner put his weapon back in the holster. "If you're lying, I'm arresting your ass."

Chris rolled his eyes. "I'll be happy for you to arrest me if we're still alive in a few hours."

They made their way through the hordes of people crowding the convention center for the symposium, everyone just milling around.

"They're all waiting for the big update coming in about five minutes," Chris explained. "To be here when it goes live gives them bragging rights."

"If they knew what it was really going to do, they wouldn't be so thrilled. Bree has been working day and night to try to find a way to stop Jeter. I have no idea if she finished."

They finally made it into any empty stairwell and started going down.

"If anybody can do it, it's Bree," Chris said. "Jeter has been obsessed with her for years, even when it seemed probable that she was dead. Melissa thought she was dead, too."

Tanner shook his head. "You know, when you said I had three hundred questions for you, that was probably a little on the conservative side."

"Get us out of this alive, and I promise I'll answer all of them. As thanks for keeping my children safe."

As they walked side by side down the hall, Tanner stuck out his hand to shake. "Deal."

Chris shook then picked up speed. "This hallway isn't used by anyone but security and food services. It leads from the main suite to the underground parking for bigwigs."

"Okay."

"The room is at the end of this hall. Our best bet is probably to try to come in an air duct from the next room or to impersonate hotel staff and get them to open—" Chris stopped to look at his phone when it beeped.

"Oh, my God." The man couldn't tear his eyes from the device.

"What?"

Chris shook his head. "That was the Communication for All update. She did it. Holy hell, did she do it."

"Bree was successful?" Not that Tanner had had much doubt.

Chris was shaking his head in awe. "She just let the whole world know what the inner circle of Communication for All was up to in the most public way possible. Every single one of those bastards will be going down."

That meant…

Tanner started running. If Jeter had Bree and knew she'd just told the world all his secrets, he would kill her for sure.

Tanner grabbed the fire extinguisher on the wall. He would use it to break down the door.

"Tanner, you don't know what the situation is like in there. You may be way outgunned."

"I don't care."

Chris pulled out a gun from the back waistband of his jeans. "Then let's do this. I'll go to the left."

Tanner brought the edge of the extinguisher down on the doorknob, feeling it rip from the jamb, then kicked it as hard as he could. Chris ran into the room, gun raised, Tanner a half step behind him.

Jeter had a gun pointed at Bree but turned at the disturbance at the door. Bree didn't waste any time. She dived at Jeter while he was distracted, Melissa jumping on top of him to help her cousin.

Chris made his own dive for the guard closest to the door, while Tanner turned and raised his weapon at Scott.

"Drop it, Scott. I don't want to have to—"

Scott's eyes narrowed, and he brought his weapon up and pointed it at Tanner.

Tanner pulled the trigger, the sound barreling through the room. Scott fell back against the wall then slid down it, eyes closed. Tanner kicked the gun away from his hand and turned.

Bree and Melissa had wrested the gun from Jeter, and Melissa was pointing it at him.

"Tanner?" Bree's green eyes were huge. "Are you okay?"

He smiled at her. "Takes more than a chubby middle school kid to stop me. Are *you* okay?"

Melissa still had the gun pointing straight at Jeter's head. "You deserve to die. For what you've done. What you were going to do."

Tanner recognized that tone. The woman was going to kill Jeter.

"Mellie, no," Bree said. "Don't. Not like this."

"He's a monster. He killed Chris."

"No, he didn't, angel." Chris moved from the guard he'd knocked unconscious. "And I'd very much like it if I didn't have to come visit my wife in prison. We've got a lot of time to make up for."

Melissa froze, looking like she couldn't believe what she was seeing. "Chris?"

She handed the gun to Bree and launched herself at him.

Jeter ignored them and looked at Bree. "You're making a mistake. We're two of the greatest technological minds of this century. Together we would be unstoppable. Think about it."

"The only thing I need to think about concerning you is that neither I nor any of my loved ones will ever be hurt by you again. And that's more than enough for me." She turned to Tanner. "Captain, will you please read Mr. Jeter his rights?"

Tanner cupped her cheek. "It would be my pleasure."

Chapter Twenty-Seven

Bree had always liked her apartment in Kansas City before. But now that she was back here, she realized how lifeless it really was.

There were no gorgeous Colorado Rockies out her window. No horses, no pregnant dogs.

There were definitely no infant twins needing constant attention and care.

Melissa and Chris had gone to California to be near his family. A family who—just like Melissa—were thrilled to discover he was alive. Melissa had invited Bree to come with them, but she'd said no.

They had a lot of lost time to make up for. A lot of memories they needed to create, just the four of them, as the sweetest nuclear family.

Bree understood that, even if it did feel a little like someone was using her heart as a pincushion. One tiny little pain after another. None of them enough to really wound her, but taken all together…agonizing.

She was free now. The Organization as it had existed was no more. After all the information came out and everyone started turning on everyone else, no one had any doubt that Jeter and all his cronies would be spending the rest of their lives in prison, although at least Ronnie Kitchens had survived.

The future of Communication for All, the actual charity, was uncertain. But maybe under the right leadership it could become great again.

Bree, or Bethany Malone, if she wanted to call herself that, was free.

No one was chasing her. Hell, she could even open a social media account if she wanted to. Make friends. Talk to other people without having to worry about being hunted.

She didn't know how to do any of those things.

So she was eating cereal at her kitchen table alone. Just like she'd started. Her spoon was halfway up to her mouth when a knock came at her door.

She didn't run for a bug-out bag this time, although she still was a little uneasy. Nobody here in the city even talked to each other. Why would someone be knocking on her door?

She looked through the peephole then fell back against the door with a thud.

Tanner.

She opened the door. "Hi."

Oh, dear. He was wearing his cowboy hat. She took in the dark hair and stark jaw that needed a shave even though it was only lunchtime. Those broad shoulders and trim waist. It had only been three weeks since she'd seen him, but she couldn't stop staring.

Finally, she met his eyes. Those soft brown eyes. "Hey there," he whispered.

"Hi." She couldn't stop her smile. She stepped back so he could come in. "What are you doing here?"

He held up a small cooler. “I brought us both a slice of Mrs. A’s lemon pie.”

She felt her eyes grow big. “Really?”

“Yep.”

She led him into the kitchen, tossing the cereal bowl in the sink and pulling out two plates. This time it was Bree who gobbled the pie down, rather than Tanner. She was already almost finished when she realized he’d barely eaten half.

“What’s wrong?”

“I want to eat it slowly. This might be the last time I get any of Mrs. Andrews’s pie.”

“Why? Are you leaving Risk Peak?” She couldn’t imagine Tanner living anywhere else.

He nodded solemnly. “Maybe. It depends.”

“On what?”

He took another small bite of his pie. “On you.”

“Me?”

“Mr. and Mrs. A said I can’t ever have another slice of their pie unless I talk you into coming back to Risk Peak.”

She smiled and swatted at him. “No, they didn’t.”

He grabbed her hand and brought it up to his lips. “Oh, they did. They miss the twins, but they miss you, too. They sent me here with that pie and told me to make sure you understood how much they—how much *all* the people of Risk Peak—want you to return. They said you could have your job back, but…” He trailed off.

She stiffened. “But what?”

He shrugged. “You’re a genius. I told them it’s beneath you to work at a job like that when you could get any job you wanted to with computers. And…" He faded off again.

She raised an eyebrow. "Have we switched bodies or something? Since when do you have trouble getting words out instead of me?"

He gave her a half grin. "I know Risk Peak isn't for everyone. It's small. You live in a big city. But I want to get to know you. Know you now when you're not an overwhelmed single mom on the run. I want to get to know the real Bree, or Bethany, or Susan. I don't care what you call yourself as long as I can be near you."

Her eyes got big. "Oh."

"If that has to be in Denver or even here, I'm willing to do that. I can put in for a job on the force here." He looked around her place, trying not to grimace. "I can make it work."

What he meant was he *would* make it work.

For her.

To be near where she was.

When she didn't want to be here at all. She wanted to be in Risk Peak.

"But there's no pie here. Or mountains. Or horses."

She could tell that she had every single bit of his attention. "No, those things aren't here. But there are computer jobs here. And you deserve the chance to live the way you want to, Bree."

"Please call me Susan."

He laughed. That sexy, confident chuckle that did things to her insides she couldn't even begin to explain. But then he grabbed both her hands.

"You're a beautiful, intelligent woman who hasn't

been given the opportunity to explore the details about herself because she's had to live in hiding."

"I want that, too. But I think I would like to try it in Risk Peak. I have no interest in working with computers right now. I might never want to again."

He shrugged. "And if so, that's okay. And I won't lie. The thought of having you in Risk Peak…everything about that feels right to me."

"You'll say whatever you have to in order to get your lemon pie privileges reinstated."

Before she could let out a squeal, she was picked up by the waist and deposited on his lap. "I'll say whatever I have to to get my *you* privileges reinstated."

She relaxed into him. She wanted that, too. "I'm new at this. I'll have to figure things out at my own pace."

"As slow as you need. For as long as you need." His lips brushed against hers with the promise of everything that could be between them.

Lips that held the promise of *home*.

* * * * *

COMING NEXT MONTH FROM

HARLEQUIN®

INTRIGUE

Available July 16, 2019

#1869 IRON WILL

Cardwell Ranch: Montana Legacy • by B.J. Daniels

Hank Savage is certain his girlfriend was murdered, so he hires private investigator Frankie Brewster to pretend to be his lover and help him find the killer. Before long, they are in over their heads...and head over heels.

#1870 THE STRANGER NEXT DOOR

A Winchester, Tennessee Thriller • by Debra Webb

After spending eight years in jail for a crime she didn't commit, Cecelia Winters is eager to find out who really killed her father, a religious fanatic and doomsday prepper. In order to discover the truth, she must work with Deacon Ross, a man who is certain Cecelia killed his mentor and partner.

#1871 SECURITY RISK

The Risk Series: A Bree and Tanner Thriller • by Janie Crouch

A few months ago, Tanner Dempsey saved Bree Daniels, but suddenly they find themselves back in danger when Tanner's past comes back to haunt the couple. Will the pair be able to stop the criminal before it's too late?

#1872 ADIRONDACK ATTACK

Protectors at Heart • by Jenna Kernan

When Detective Dalton Stevens follows his estranged wife, Erin, to the Adirondack Mountains in an effort to win her back, neither of them expects to become embroiled in international intrigue. Then they are charged with delivering classified information to Homeland Security.

#1873 PERSONAL PROTECTION

by Julie Miller

Ivan Mostek knows two things: someone wants him dead and a member of his inner circle is betraying him. With undercover cop Carly Valentine by his side, can he discover the identity of the traitor before it's too late?

#1874 NEW ORLEANS NOIR

by Joanna Wayne

Helena Cosworth is back in New Orleans to sell her grandmother's house. Suddenly, she is a serial killer's next target, and she is forced to turn to Detective Hunter Bergeron, a man she once loved and lost, for help. Together, will they be able to stop the elusive French Kiss Killer?

Three years ago, Deputy Tanner Dempsey was involved in a mission that went wrong. Now, trying to keep his PTSD under control while he falls deeper for Bree Daniels, his past returns, threatening the life he thought was finally back on track...

Read on for a sneak peek at
Security Risk,
from USA TODAY *bestselling author Janie Crouch.*

It wasn't long before they were arriving at the ranch. He grabbed her overnight bag, and they walked inside.

"We both need to get a few hours' sleep," he said. "I'll take the couch and you can have the bed."

She walked toward the bedroom but turned at the door. "Come with me. Just to sleep together like before." Those big green eyes studied him as she reached her hand out toward him.

There was nothing he wanted more than to curl up with her in his bed. But with his anger and frustration so close to the surface, he couldn't discount the fact that he might wake up swinging. The thought of Bree being the recipient of his night terrors made him break out into a cold sweat.

"Never mind," she said quickly, misreading his hesitation, hand falling back to her side. "You don't have to."

Damn it, he'd rather never sleep again than see that wounded look in her eyes from something he'd done.

He stepped toward her. "I want to. Trust me, there's nothing I want more. But…I just don't want to take a chance on waking you up if I get called back in to Risk Peak early." That was at least a partial truth.

The haunted look fell away from her eyes, and a shy smile broke on her face. "I don't mind. I'll take a shorter amount of sleep if it means I get to sleep next to you."

He would have given her anything in the world to keep that sweet smile on her face. He took her hand, and they walked into the bedroom together.

They took turns changing into sleep clothes in the bathroom, then got into the bed together. The act was so innocent and yet so intimate.

Tanner rolled over onto his side and pulled Bree's back against his front. He breathed in the sweet scent of her hair as her head rested in the crook of his elbow. His other arm wrapped loosely around her waist.

She was out within minutes, her smaller body relaxing against him, trusting him to shelter and protect her while she slept. Tanner wouldn't betray that trust, even if that meant protecting her against himself.

Besides, sleeping was overrated when he could be awake and feeling every curve that had been haunting his dreams for months pressed against him.

Definitely worth it.

SPECIAL EXCERPT FROM

In order to clean up his player reputation, rodeo champ and cowboy Nico Laramie asks his best friend, Eden Joslin, to pretend they're an exclusive couple. But one kiss with the woman he's always kept at a distance and Nico knows this fake relationship is about to turn into something very real...

Read on for a sneak peak at
Sweet Summer Sunset
part of the Coldwater Texas series from
USA TODAY *bestselling author Delores Fossen.*

"You've been avoiding me," Eden added, and she set the grocery bags on the small kitchen counter.

"I have," he admitted, and he wanted to wince. This was the problem with crossing a line with a friend. He wasn't used to putting on mouth filters when it came to Eden. "I wanted to give us both some time."

Her eyebrow came up, and she huffed before she mumbled some frustrated profanity under her breath.

"See?" he snapped, as if that proved all the arguments going on in his head. "We're uncomfortable with each other, and it's all because of the kiss that shouldn't have happened."

She stared at him a moment, caught on to a handful of his shirt and yanked him to her. She kissed him. Hard.

Nico felt his body jolt, an involuntary reaction that nearly made him dive in for more. After all, good kisses should be deep and involve some tongue. It was like stripping off a layer of clothes or going to the next level. But those were places that Nico stopped himself from going. Before their tongues could get involved, he

PHDFEXP0719

stepped back from her, and she let go of him, her grip melting off his shirt.

He felt the loss right away when her mouth was no longer on his. The loss and the realization that Eden was a real, live, breathing woman. An attractive one with breasts, legs and everything.

Oh man.

He didn't want to realize that. He wanted his friend. And he wanted that friendship almost as much as he wanted to French-kiss her.

"Now we can also be uncomfortable because of that kiss I just gave you," she said, as if that proved whatever point she'd been trying to make. It proved nothing. Well, nothing that should be proved anyway.

Nico stared at her. "Eden, you're playing with a thousand gallons of fire," he warned her—after he'd caught his breath.

"I know, and I'm going to be honest about that. In fact, I'm going to insist we be honest with each other so that we don't ruin our friendship."

That was very confusing, and Nico wondered if this was some kind of trick. Except Eden wasn't a trick-playing kind of person. "What the heck do you mean by that?"

Her gaze stayed level with his. "It means if you want to kiss me, you should. If you don't want to kiss me again, then don't."

He was still confused. About what she was saying anyway. Nico was reasonably sure that the wanting-to-kiss-her part was highly charged right now.

"I just don't want you to avoid me because you're struggling with this possible curveball that's been tossed into our friendship," Eden went on. "That kiss makes us even," she added with a firm nod.

Don't miss
Sweet Summer Sunset *by Delores Fossen,*
available July 2019 wherever HQN books
and ebooks are sold.

www.Harlequin.com

PHDFEXP0719